From the bunker, Sgt. Mike Reider looked toward the flaming HQ and hissed at Lt. Williams, "Do you see what I see?"

Williams followed the look. "That dirty—! It's Lim. That son of a bitch. He's sold us out!"

Williams started to sight on the traitor with his M-16, but Reider stopped him. "If you take him out now, it'll blow our position."

Reider would regret that decision. For Lim would take him prisoner, and would begin trying with every means to break the Beret's spirit.

Reider was determined that Lim should fail. . . .

CRY HAVOC

BARRY SADLER

TOR

A TOM DOHERTY ASSOCIATES BOOK

"The Ballad of the Green Berets" is copyright©1963, 1964, 1966 by Music, Music, Music, Inc. Reprinted by permission.

A Tor Book

Published by Tom Doherty Associates, 8-10 W. 36th St., New York, New York 10018

First printing, June 1983

ISBN: 0-523-48057-1

Printed in the United States of America

Distributed by Pinnacle Books, 1430 Broadway, New York, New York 10018

*Cry havoc,
and let loose the dogs of war. . . .*

Fighting soldiers from the sky,
Fearless men who jump and die.
Men who mean just what they say,
The brave men of the Green Beret.
Silver wings upon their chests,
These are men, America's best,
One hundred men we'll test today,
But only three win the Green Beret.

Trained to live off nature's land
Trained to combat, hand to hand.
Men who fight by night and day,
Courage take from the Green Beret.
Silver wings upon their chests,
These are men, America's best,
One hundred men we'll test today,
But only three win the Green Beret.

Back at home a young wife waits,
Her Green Beret has met his fate.
He has died for those oppressed,
Leaving her this last request.
Put silver wings on my son's chest,
Make him one of America's best,
He'll be a man they'll test one day,
Have him win the Green Beret.

CRY HAVOC

CHAPTER ONE

The scurrying of rats over and under the palm logs and sandbags in the dank bunker scratched against his nerves. A single short candle flickered from its resting place in a year-old sardine tin. Reider turned over on his side to watch the dancing shadows of the candle on the wall of his close, dark cavern. Near to hand were his rifle and combat pack, stuffed with extra ammo, grenades, and a few rations. Several of the logs were sprouting green broad-leafed shoots like those of rubber trees. They kept forcing their way out of the decaying bark in a futile quest for sunlight; he had to trim the leaves back every couple of weeks.

His salt sores itched where his fatigue trousers had been too tight. The calamine lotion Mac had given him wasn't doing much good; the itching made it hard to sleep, but then it was always hard to sleep unless you were blind drunk, and even then, you stood a better than even chance of waking up dead. Dead! Was it all that bad? There were worse things than being dead. There was pain. Pain that couldn't be put into words. Pain that ate at your soul, trying to vomit out of your guts, up through your mouth into a mindless cry of agony that had no beginning or end. It only faded dimly, into the canyons of distance and time, but it was always there, waiting. A word, sound, or smell could trigger it into flames again, to burn as fresh as it did when first felt.

Dead definitely was not the worst of things that could happen to a man. Death was expected, even normal. Every day people died by the tens of thousands, and here death walked with you constantly. The Republic of South Vietnam was not a great place for insurance actuaries to ply their percentage points.

Reider reached over to a moldy 60mm ammo box that served as his table. Shoving aside the forty-five automatic with a round in the chamber, he poured a short shot of Jim Beam, resisting the temptation to fill the water glass to the brim. You don't get drunk in the field. Save that for a trip to

Pleiku. He had one coming up soon; then he could lay it on. Raising the dirty glass up to the candle, he looked through it, moving the amber liquid back and forth, watching the play of light through it. The movement was pleasing to watch. It calmed the nerves a bit, like petting a dog. Opening his mouth, he slowly sipped the whiskey. Holding it between his lips and gums, he rolled it around, letting the semisweet astringent clean the night scum from his mouth; then he let it slide slowly down his throat. It settled with a familiar warm glow.

Putting down the empty glass, he wet his forefinger and winked out the candle. He took the forty-five from the table, and holding it limply in his hand, finger off the trigger, he lay back on the grey-stained pillow.

A strip of camouflage parachute served as a curtain between him and the outside passage that led to the mortar pits and ammo room; from beyond it a bare sixty-watt bulb glowed, its light pulsating with the shifting of the diesel generator fifty yards away. That light and the thin curtain were his warning signals. If anything passed in front of the light for even a heart beat, his eyes would click open, instantly focusing, as they did a dozen times a night, every time the generator coughed.

This was the worst part, lying there waiting, knowing that some of your own troops topside were Viet Cong. How many, you couldn't tell, but as sure as death some up there were just waiting for the word to toss a grenade in your hooch or put a burst from a submachine gun in your back at breakfast or on guard duty. That was the worst part of this kind of work. For two months, he hadn't taken his boots or trousers off at night, or slept without the pistol in his hand. They'd come some time; it was just a matter of when. He wanted to scratch between his toes where a patch of fungus was doing its best to turn into jungle rot from the constant sweat and dampness.

The generator shifted and the passage light faded for a second, then came back to strength. Mindlessly, his finger moved to the trigger of his pistol and his thumb to the hammer, which was already on half-cock. He wanted to sleep, but it wouldn't come. In a couple of hours he would have to go watch, taking a place in one of the machine-gun bunkers. Till then he knew he would do as he had for the last week, just lie there and fight his mind. Try to erase memories that he knew were his fault but ached in a manner that ate at him, slow, acid, worse than a quick kill. Still, it had been his fault. Twisting onto his side, he moved the pistol across his chest, smelling the light sweetness of the gun oil. He let the cooler steel touch him, sliding along against the clammy skin of his stomach to rest half against him and half on the dark blankets.

If he'd only let her have a little warning that he was coming home early, it might never have happened. But he was going to surprise her. Her big tough hero was coming home to his loving wife. Shit! Hero? Green Beret? Fearless soldier? The son of a bitch that wrote those lines must have been talking about a different army. He had known fear but nothing like the fear when he had opened the door to his bedroom and saw—what was it the poet called it? "The beast with two backs"? He'd just stood there for a second, the blood draining from his face, looking over the man's shoulder at her. He'd felt something drop out of his guts. She didn't say anything, just lay there looking at him while the man on top of her ground his hips, thrusting into her. He saw the fear in her face. The thought of killing them came first. It would have been easy; he knew all the tricks of the trade; but he couldn't. Something had already died, and it was in him. He didn't want to see who the man was. If the man turned around, then he might kill him. He didn't want to know. He didn't want another face to live with. The tough guy couldn't even kill the son of a bitch that was screwing his wife while he watched.

He had just turned around and gone out the door. Why he hadn't killed them he didn't know then. It was later, at the Shangri-la bar on Yadkin road, that his good friends Jack Daniels and Jim Beam helped him find some answers. They may not have been the right ones, but they were better than none.

Why the hell should she have been saving it for him? He damned sure hadn't saved anything. The old double standard—it was all right for the man but not the woman. And he'd been overseas more time than he'd been at home. Months had run into years, with him gone and her never knowing if he was going to come back without legs, arms, or in a box. It had never been a real marriage, no kids. Maybe that would have made a difference, but he doubted it. If he had stayed home, gotten out of the Army, and taken a 9-to-5, it would have destroyed him. He'd been in too long to change. The Army was all he knew; it was home. Not his house or his wife—they were just something he came to when the Army didn't need him for a few hours or days. The Army was mistress and home. His wife had had to take third or fourth place in his list of priorities.

The generator farted again, the faint smell of diesel fumes drifting to him. He had done the honorable thing; he had run away again. She filed for divorce (irreconcilable differences); he didn't contest it. He never said another word to her. He wondered why it hurt so much. He'd known it was bound to happen sometime. The loving had stopped a long time ago, and there had never been any sharing. She had always been an outsider. Was it just his pride that hurt? It shouldn't have mattered. After all, this was the twentieth century. People were supposed to be more sophisticated about such matters.

His Commanding Officer, Col. Ahearn, knew he had a problem. He didn't know the details, but he knew what was needed to help cure it. He'd okayed Reider for another tour to Nam before he was due. Now he was back, and it was helping. Here, everything was familiar, easy to understand. And the threat of death at any moment was enough to keep the memories pushed to the back most of the time. That was the beauty of the service. It was simple. You knew where you stood and what was expected of you, and you didn't have to make complicated decisions that hurt you where you lived. He knew that most of the men serving in his team with him felt the same way. Especially old Sizemore, the team sergeant. It was rumored that he had olive-drab blood in his veins. People like him and Sizemore would have a hard time adjusting when the day came for them to retire, providing, of course, they lived that long. They just didn't really fit anywhere, except someplace like this. He'd seen enough oldtimers at Bragg or Benning that couldn't adjust, hanging around the VFW or American Legion club drinking their lives away, trying to capture their past again, talking to others like themselves: "Do you remember when. . . ." That's all he would have left. He would never really belong to the outside world and didn't want to.

He didn't like civilians; he had nothing in common with them. He didn't like their clothes. He didn't like their faces. He didn't like them! And he knew they felt the same way about him, and that was all right, too. He knew you couldn't trust civilians. The enemy was more reliable, more worthy of respect, because he was doing the same damned job as you with the same problems and feelings; he just wore a different uniform. Politics and ideologies were for civilians, not soldiers. Families were

for civilians, 9-to-5 was for civilians, and so was
his goddamned wife! He knew that, because the
son of a bitch in bed with her had needed a hair-
cut!

The weight of the perforated steel plating overhead under its mixed layers of logs and dirt, and
cap of rotting sandbags, seemed suddenly very
heavy, oppressive. It was hard to breath. Piss on
it! Resisting the temptation to pour another shot,
he put on his jacket, grabbed his combat pack and
rifle, and started topside. So what if he was a bit
early? No one would give a shit. At least he could
watch the darkness. He didn't like being down in
the bunker, it was too much like a trap. Outside
was always better, unless Charley was lobbing in
some mortar rounds or 122mm rockets at your
ass. He'd go ahead and wait for Lt. Williams to
join him. A few more minutes and they could get
to the night's work.

Walking across the inner compound, trying to
avoid tripping over the wire stabilizing lines that
secured the radio antennas, he could see faint
glows of light through the ground fog that had
rolled up from the river bed. He knew that Captain
Robbins was in the commo room as usual; across
an apron of concertina wire, a dim hazy orange
glow came from the room of the South Vietnamese
commander, Robbins' counterpart, Captain (or as
the Vietnamese would say, Dai Ui) Lim. He wondered why the Vietnamese officer was still up so
late. Maybe he had his problems too.

By the time he reached the machinegun bunker,

he had himself back together. He had something to hold onto, he had an identity. He was a soldier! That was it, and it was enough. It couldn't be taken away from him; he could hold onto it; it was his rock, his reason for being. It was good, clean, honest. . . .

Shoving the flap open, he went down the four steps into the bunker, telling the two Viets there to take off and get some shuteye, he'd handle things now.

CHAPTER TWO

Captain Lim, commanding the Luc Luong Dac Biet, the South Vietnamese counterparts of the American Special Forces, at the camp of Plei Jrong, checked his Rolex for the tenth time in as many minutes. Outside his room the familiar damp of a night fog rested over the camp.

Soon. It would happen soon. The familiar sensation of anxiety and fear mixed with anticipation came over him. He removed his U.S. Army issue forty-five from its holster, checked the magazine, then jacked a round into the chamber. At his hip, in a smooth leather scabbard, was the comforting weight of his bowie knife with the Special Forces crest engraved on it. It had been given to him by Captain Chandler as a memento of the many missions they had shared over the last year. Chandler would be rotating soon; he only had three more days in camp.

He picked up his weapon, a vintage WWII M2 carbine, loaded with two thirty-round banana clips, held together with a broad strip of green tape. The carbine was a comfortable, easy shooting rifle which he favored over the M-16. Gathering up a bag of grenades to sling over his left shoulder, he caught a look at his face in the small mirror hanging near a crucifix on the wall of his room. It was, he thought, a good face. He examined his reflection carefully, as he did at least once every day, searching for any tell-tale signs of weakness. The jawline was firm; there was just a touch of grey at the temples; the brown eyes looked intelligent and the mouth determined. He knew he looked the part of a dedicated professional soldier and had always made certain his superiors thought so too.

Turning down the Coleman lantern plunged his room into sudden and startling darkness. The 8x8 space in the back of the LLDB HQ that served as his private quarters for the last two years felt oppressive when the light went out, as if the weight of the dozens of hard crusty sandbags on its roof and along its sides were about to break through the palm log rafters and crush him.

He could have had one of the rooms in the underground bunkers, but he had refused it. He had never liked being closed in. Lim shook his head as he put on his camouflage soft cap. There was no time for such thoughts; he had to keep his mind clear. Outside the perimeters of Plei Jrong were two battalions of the 126th PVN, from one of the best VC main force regiments. Things could get very sticky before this night was through.

As he left the close room, it felt good to catch the first breath of air outside. The fog gave it a trace of coolness.

The camp was cloaked in shadows. Lim knew that outside the hundred or so meters where bush had been hacked away to provide clear fields of fire, one was back in the stone age. In that sometimes heaving mass of foliage, killers hunted, and not all were of the four-legged variety. Inside the triple apron of mines, barricades, barbed wire and tangle-foot, the bunkers showed only as darker forms in the night. The antennas of the commo room stuck up over the humped black forms of the log and bamboo barracks for the Strikers—two companies of Vietnamese and one of Montagnards from the Jarai tribe. Moi, thought Lim. Like most Vietnamese, he held the hill people in contempt.

There were normally twelve American advisors in the camp, but two of them had gone into Pleiku—the senior medic, Mac Rigsby, and Master Sergeant Sizemore, the intelligence and operations sergeant. The eleven Vietnamese of his own

LLDB made up the rest of the complement of this small outpost stuck near the Cambodian border, where the next friendly installation was over forty miles away.

Lim sucked in another deep breath, resisting the temptation to light up one of the Winston cigarettes Chandler had given him. The two men had much in common. They had earned their small outpost a reputation that was the envy of many larger installations in the central highlands. Both had been decorated for gallantry by the SV government several times. They were very, very much alike in many ways.

He knew this camp better than he did any place in the world. He knew every shack and bunker, every gun emplacement and guard post. He knew who was on the guard posts, and who was in the rack.

He was not one to leave such details to a junior officer. He had always known that one night the knowledge would be vital. Tonight was that night. He wondered how his countrymen outside the barbed wire, in the jungle, felt about what they were going to attempt. About killing those of their own blood. And would he himself feel any different than he had in the past, when he had taken the lives of his own race in the name of duty?

Everything was normal. He shivered, a mixture of chill and anticipation for that which was to come.

A quiet shadow joined him. His adjutant, Chung Ui Van Minh. Even in the dark Lim could see the gleam of anticipation in his dark moist eyes.

"Be patient," he whispered. "It won't be much longer. Have you alerted our men?"

Van responded with confidence in his young voice: "Quyet-team chien." All was well, everything was ready.

Lim gave him permission to continue with his duties. He was very pleased with the handsome young lieutenant of a good family, from An Giang in the 4th Military Sector. Van had progressed rapidly. He was completely loyal, something one could not always be certain of, in these troubled times. There were traitors and informers everywhere. Van was swallowed by the mist as he moved away.

Lim checked his watch again. Four minutes to three. It would be at least three more hours before dawn. This was the kind of night the VC favored for an attack; when visibility was nil. They would be able to get very close to the first apron of wire before being detected. He wanted a cigarette to ease the tremor in his hands.

Climbing up a pile of sandbags arranged as steps, he reached the top of the commo bunker, where his head was above the level of the ground fog. In the distance he saw, for a brief moment, a flash in the sky. Heat lightning! It broke behind the ridge of mountains to the west, rippling and wavering, then was gone. Was it an omen from the Than Tien, the spirits of the mountains?

It was nearly time. He climbed back down the sandbags moving towards the tin-roofed shack

that served as the HQ for the Special Forces team.
He knew Chandler was on duty tonight, probably
staying close to their backup radio, listening to the
Armed Forces Radio broadcast from Saigon.

He could hear the small noises of unseen others,
the familiar muffled sounds of men on watch: a
rifle bolt being worked to check the action, a
cough from a machinegun bunker near the south
corner. Above them all, in the tower, was a spot-
light manned by two Strikers from the Montagnard company, standing ready to light up fire
zones when needed.

He wondered how the Americans were going to
react. They were good, he had to admit that, even
if they really didn't have any true interest in his
country. They were damned good soldiers. But
they could never know the feelings he had for this
land of his ancestors. They were only fighters,
with no understanding of him and his countrymen. No understanding of Chet vinh hon song
nhuc, an honorable death rather than a shameful
life.

A thin bright glow came from under the door to
the Americans' HQ, and then unpleasant strains of
what the bignoses called music filtering out into
the mist. His guess about Chandler's whereabouts
had been correct. Opening the door, Lim slid
inside quickly, closing it behind him.

Chandler turned from the plank table near the
radio, a pleased smile coming to his face when he
saw Lim. He let the hammer fall back easy on his
9mm Browning Hi-Power, setting the pistol back
on the table.

"What the hell are you doing up this late? You don't have watch tonight."

Lim shrugged his shoulders. "I don't feel easy tonight. I think something's going to happen."

Chandler stood up, raising his arms over his head to stretch out the kinks in his back. He eyeballed his friend. Lim had been right too many times in the past for Chandler not to take his feelings seriously. "Okay, buddy, you tell me! It's been quiet for weeks around here. What do you think is going to happen?"

Lim moved closer to him. Chandler's eyes went wide. He tried to speak but couldn't. The gaping wound in his throat prevented the air in his lungs from reaching his vocal cords. Another swift firm hack nearly took his head off, leaving his eyes with a confused, slightly bewildered look before they glazed over and Lim let his body fall to the dusty floor.

Wiping the blood off the blade of the bowie knife, Lim responded quietly to Captain Chandler's last question. "I think you are going to die."

He moved Chandler out of sight to a corner by the radio, where he covered him up with one of the rough red-and-black striped Montagnard blankets. Now it was time for the other two asleep in the building to be taken care of. Silently he eased down the passage leading from the rear of the hut to where the junior medic and the heavy weapons man lay in silence that would soon be eternal.

He visited each man for just a moment. That

was all the time it took to cover the Americans'
mouths, to let the thick blade and razor edge of the
bowie knife flash briefly in the dim light. Then it
was over. Three down, seven to go.

For years he had been waiting for this day. It
was very satisfying at last to be true to himself. He
looked at his watch once more. He had only a few
minutes before his comrades outside would move
on the camp; he had to be ready. If only it wasn't
for those filthy savages, the Montagnards, he
would be assured of easy going. One full company
of the strike force were loyal comrades that he had
personally recruited, and one by one assigned to
the same unit. Every man there was one of his. But
there was no way he could infiltrate the Montagnards; they were distrustful of all Vietnamese,
North or South. But the Americans were the
brains of the traitorous Viet company and the
savages. Once they were removed, his comrades
outside the wire and his men inside should have
few difficulties in taking the camp.

He wondered how his lieutenant was making
out. By now Chung Ui Van Minh would have been
joined by the other two loyal comrades in the
LLDB and one sent to give the order to Houng,
commander of the Viet strike force. Each of
Houng's Strikers knew what he would have to do
this night.

The nine members of Lim's team who were loyal
to the SV regime of Premier Thieu, would by now
have been killed quickly in their sleep by the
knives of Houng's Strikers; the rest of them

should now be at their positions, waiting for the signal.

Lim left the HQ after removing the crystal from the radio. He might have need for it later; the Viet Cong were always short of communications equipment. Now to take care of the rest of the A Team. They were spread out around the camp. As he started across the compound, he saw that his men under the command of Houng and Van were already breaking up into separate units. One unit was moving into position around the Mon barracks, setting up two 30-caliber machineguns. A third of their company was waiting to take care of any survivors that might try to break out of the thatch building after the shooting started. Another third were doing the same to the Vietnamese company.

Some of their men were on the wall, as were soldiers from each of the other two companies. He had tried to talk Captain Chandler into having the watch rotated each night by company so that on this night he would have the only men on guard and could have control of all vital placements. But the American hadn't bought it. And Lim had known that to push the issue would invite suspicions.

The tricky part was coming now. He had to dispose of the Americans on watch, and sleeping in areas where Montagnard guards were posted. He would try to take them out himself, as they all knew him and trusted his loyalty to the Thieu regime.

He had made it a point to gain their confidence, and nearly made himself ill with playing at being their good and devoted friend. When they went into Pleiku on convoy or R&R he gave them numbers to call that always produced pretty, clean girls to take care of them. If they needed cash, he knew where they could get the best rates on the black-market; he even arranged for them to buy sapphires and gold at below market prices. Lim had indeed been a valued friend to them during their stay in his country. Now he would be their executioner. It was a role decidedly more to his liking.

He had to hurry. There were only ten minutes left, and a thousand things could yet go wrong.

CHAPTER THREE

   As Lim began to hurry, a sudden cry from the Montagnard barracks was followed by a sustained burst of full automatic fire from a .45-caliber sub-machinegun. Lim cursed. His attackers had been spotted too soon. A panic of confusion followed. The camp mortars began sending up illuminating rounds, breaking the night into a burst of eye-searing white brilliance. The men on the walls and in the bunkers didn't know where to fire. There was nothing in front of them; all the firing and the sounds of fighting were coming from their rear.

Lim's company of infiltrators were hitting their assigned targets. The dull thumps of grenades going off in sleeping quarters and in machinegun bunkers accented the sharper chatter of rifle fire.

Lim shifted his carbine to the ready as he moved to the entrance of the bunker on the northeast corner. SP-5 Johnston, the junior communications man, stood in the trench connecting the bunker with the other perimeter defenses. He spotted Lim running towards him.

"Hurry up, Captain," he cried to Lim, waving him on.

A three-round burst from the carbine blew Johnston's lower jaw off, the copper-jacketed bullets pushing through and out the back of the skull. Then Lim was over Johnston's body and inside the bunker, emptying the rest of his thirty-round magazine in the backs of the other two Americans who had their eyes to the front, looking out the firing slit towards the barbed wire, the direction they thought the attack would come from. Sergeants Murphy and Ziebart, the demo men, never knew what hit them.

Releasing the empty mag, Lim slapped in a full one and recocked his piece. Now, where were the other four so-called advisors? He came out of the entrance to the bunker and raised his head to survey the action inside the walls. A burst from an M-16 ripped up the sandbag directly in front of him. Bits of canvas and sand nearly took out his left eye.

Lieutenant Williams and Reider were outside their bunker to the front when the surprise attack took place. They'd been laying some line leading to a new apron of claymore mines they had just set out behind the inner roll of tanglefoot wire set on their side of the punji stake ditch, using the cover of darkness and the faded black-striped pattern of their camouflage fatigues to keep their activities from the ever-watchful eyes in the jungle surrounding them.

The Jarai tribesman, in the bunker behind them, died seconds after the first shots took place around the Montagnard barracks. He stuck his head out of his hole and lost it to a blast from a twelve-gauge riot gun. A grenade was then thrown into the bunker to finish off the two Americans the infiltrators thought were inside.

After the grenade went off, Williams and Reider crawled back in the bunker. Checking the machine gun, they found it still in operating condition. But the direct phone line connection them to HQ and the other positions was out. They didn't know what was happening or who had been hit. What they did know was that something was god-damned sure rotten, and it wasn't in Denmark.

Kosun, the Montagnards' company commander, was walking the guard posts by himself, just doing a little checking to make certain none of his people were falling down on the job, when he spotted the Viets setting up around his barracks.

He had great pride in his abilities as a soldier, having fought against the Viet Minh with the French for four years before being captured at Dien Bien Phu. The three months he was their prisoner before being released as part of the truce agreement gave him memories that forever put communists on the top of his kill list.

When he spotted the Viet gunners setting up, he knew immediately what was taking place. There was no time to warn anyone, for he was spotted only a second after he saw them. The best warning would be if he could just wake everyone up.

A full burst from his M-3 submachinegun ripped up the machinegun crew and woke nearly twenty of his men in time to break out of their shack before the other Viets could get the gun working again.

Rallying his surviving Strikers, Kosun moved on a bunker and mortar pit and killed the Vietnamese there. Not knowing whether they were friendly or not, he didn't take time to ask. Right now all Viets other than his Strikers were enemies until proven otherwise.

Once the flares from the mortars went up and the sounds of heavy fighting reached the eyes and ears in the jungle, the VC made their move, even thought it was still two minutes to their scheduled jump-off time. They hit the main gate with sappers loaded down with stachel charges and bangalore torpedoes to blast an opening. The VC outside laid enough fire on the rest of the camp to keep the remaining defenders tied down in their positions.

Kosun saw Jenkins, the black senior commo sergeant, and First Sgt. Vidreen, the senior NCO,
being dragged out of a 60mm mortar pit. They had
jumped into it expecting to find a friendly crew,
but had met instead, Lt. Van and five of Lim's infiltrators. Van wasted no time on them. They were
bayoneted and shot repeatedly, with no chance to
defend themselves.

That left only Williams and Reider.

Kosun's remaining Strikers were giving a good
account of themselves. They had gotten the
mortar in their pit working and were throwing
rounds all over the camp, firing nearly straight up
with no extra charges, to make certain the shells
would land inside their own perimeters. They had
also begun to lay down light weapons fire both
inside and outside the camp.

Fires were breaking out, adding a sick red glow
to the mist hovering over the camp, mixing smoke
and cordite with the damp. The commo room was
on fire, as were most of the barracks. The supply
huts and dispensary were untouched; The VC
needed what was in them for their own use.

One of Kosun's mortars hit the POL squarely
with a white phosphorus round, setting off the
drums of diesel fuel and gasoline. Explosions
rocked the ground, drowning out for a second the
sounds of machineguns and the screams of
wounded and dying men.

Kosun could see about sixty Cong gathering

near the burning HQ for an assault on his small strong point. It was difficult to spread his men thin enough to cover all that was coming at them from three sides. His twenty Strikers were now reduced to sixteen who could still fight; the others were either dead or too badly wounded to be of any use.

Lim had broken free from whoever it was that had shot at him, using as cover a cloud of thick oily smoke that rolled his way when the fuel depot had gone up. He rejoined Van and his main force as the gates were blasted open and over a hundred Bo Doi of the People's Army of Liberation rushed inside.

The Vietnamese company had lain down their arms after the first burst of machine gun raked their barracks. Only a few still held their ground in individual foxholes around the camp. It was those damned Moi that were holding up everything. They were taking out entirely too many of Lim's men with that damned mortar, and their rifle fire was keeping too many pinned down. He gathered up his force to make an assault. The Viet Cong in the camp would give him covering fire once they were in place.

Reider and Williams were keeping low, trying to figure out what was happening and who was left alive. In the light of the fires they saw the bodies of their friends being dragged out by the heels and left in front of the mess hall. They tried to make a count, but couldn't tell whether the Cong had got them all.

The only resistance seemed to be coming from the region of mortar pit 3. That meant that at least some of their people were still holding out, though Reider didn't think they could last much longer, and there was little likelihood that any help could reach them in time. With the radios gone and their "check-in" call not due for another five minutes, it would be impossible for a reaction force to get in here from Pleiku before the camp was completely overrun.

The Cong were ignoring the mines and wire surrounding the camp; they had an open door now in the front gate. There was still a fair amount of small arms fire coming at the camp from the tree-line. A couple of squads must have been left there as security, Reider figured.

Reider looked toward the flaming HQ and hissed at Williams, "Do you see what I see?"

Williams followed the look. "That dirty motherfucker! It's Lim. That son of a bitch! He's sold us out."

Williams started to sight on the traitor with his M-16, but Reider stopped him, pointing toward the firing coming from mortar pit 3. "We've still got some people out there, and it looks like he's going to hit them. If you take him out now, it'll blow out position. Wait until they get bunched up. When they start moving, then we'll give it to them." Reluctantly, Williams agreed.

They pulled the machinegun out of the bunker,

setting it up where they would have a good field of
fire at the backs of the Viets. The Viets would have
to cross an open space of about forty yards when
they assaulted the Montagnards.

Lim gave Van his orders. The young lieutenant
would have the honor of eliminating the last resistance in Plei Jrong. Lim would remain behind
with a Viet Cong captain who had entered the
camp and was now requesting the location of the
weapons and supplies they were to take back with
them.

The VC regulars laid down a withering barrage
of fire on the Montagnards, killing four in the first
five seconds, forcing the others to keep their heads
down or lose them. Van gave the order, and his
men rushed across the open space. They would be
on the Jarais in less than twenty seconds. But, in
combat, seconds can mean a hundred lifetimes.

The M-60 in Williams' hands cut loose, over six
hundred rounds a minute rattling out of its
muzzle, every fifth round a tracer to guide by. Williams was a damned fine machinegunner. At this
distance, with an open field of fire and the targets
packed tight, there was no way he could miss. Sixteen of the Viets went down in four seconds, most
with stomachs dangling entrails where the 7.62
bullets had burst them open on their way out. That
four seconds was enough to halt the initial
impetus of the assault. The Viets hit the ground.
The next four brought more death and confusion
as Williams then turned his gun on the far side of

the camp against the Cong, keeping them down.

Reider rose up high enough to yell to the Montagnards. "Is that you, Kosun?"

Kosun's dark eyes sparkled as he yelled back, "Yes!" There were Americans left alive, and his good friend and brother, Trung Si Reider, was one of them.

"Get your ass over here, we'll cover you."

Kosun needed no more encouragement. He and his men burst out of the bunker and mortar pit, pausing only to put bullets into the brains of the wounded who couldn't go with them. It was an act of mercy; they knew the fate of those taken alive by the VC.

As Williams did his best to burn up the barrel of his machinegun, Reider gave what support he could with his rifle, taking out three of the Bo Doi who had bunched up too close together. The Jarais reached them, losing only three men killed and two with minor wounds. They piled on top of each other as they hit the trench, scrambling to the right and left to take up firing positions.

Kosun slid in along side Reider, breathless. There was not a trace of fear in that dark, almost Indian face. He had walked with death too many times to be afraid of that which comes to all. "Baissez la téte, Sergent!"

Reider growled, "How the fuck am I going to keep my head down and shoot at the same time, dumb shit?"

Kosun gave an excellent imitation of the classic Gallic shrug he'd learned while with the Foreign

Legion. It was also where he had learned to speak French. If it was a good enough language for L'Etrange, the Legion, then it should be good enough for all bignoses no matter where they came from. Besides, he knew it irritated Reider, who had more or less adopted him a couple of years before. He would come to him for orders even if there was another American around who outranked his roundeyed friend. This used to piss Captain Chandler off a bit. Which was one of the reasons he did it.

Williams yelled over the roar of the machinegun to Kosun. "Did you see any more GI's?"

Kosun drew down and killed the VC captain who had been standing by Lim, before telling them that Vidreen and Jenkins had been butchered.

Williams cursed between clenched teeth as he ran through another belt of ammo. "Well, I guess we're it, then. What say we get the fuck out of here while we still can?" He received no objections to that from anyone.

On each side of the camp there was a narrow safe path out through the mines, leading to spots where the wire wasn't staked down as tight as it should be. Only the Americans knew of these exits; they had built them themselves for just such an emergency. It was known that nearly every Special Forces camp that had fallen, had been taken with inside help. The exit builders had strict orders to tell no one; not even the most trusted of Vietnamese or Montagnards knew the locations of the safe routes.

Inside the machinegun bunker were some cases of smoke grenades, as there were in every bunker. Williams told Reider to get them ready and take the lead; he'd continue to give cover. Then Reider was to do the same for him when he broke away.

Reider readied the grenades; then they tossed them out in all directions, blocking the view of the Viet gunners.

There were by now only eleven men to lead out. Reider led the way, each man staying close behind the one in front of him. Running, then crawling, as the situation dictated, they wormed and wriggled their way through the three aprons of wire, across the punji stake pit and under the eight-foot-tall barbed wire fence, the first of two encircling Plei Jrong. There Reider halted and, pointing out to Kosun the path to follow, let the Yards go on ahead.

He yelled for Williams to cut loose and get his tail out of there. Williams gave one last long hosing spread with the M-60, then disappeared into the smoke. Reider wanted to fire but didn't. It would have brought too much return fire back on him. It was best to let the smoke hide them and just hope they would be able to get clear before it blew away.

Williams nearly knocked Reider down when he ran past him, leaping over a four-foot wall of concertina like an Olympic athlete, yelling back, "What the shit are you waiting for?"

Kosun and his Strikers were already clear of the camp and were taking out the few Viets in the woods directly to their front by the time the two Americans reached them. Without stopping, they all took to the woods, crashing through the brush, ignoring vines and branches that tried to poke their eyes out. Behind them the flames of the camp lit up the night sky, but the dense under-brush and thick trees muffled the sounds as ammunition caught fire and exploded in the burning barracks.

They were in the clear for the time being. By now the B Team at Pleiku would be sending out spotter aircraft to see why the camp hadn't made its "check-in" call. Once the fires were seen it wouldn't be long before an airstrike was on the way and a Mike Force behind it. Several spots had been preselected for a rendezvous if the camp was overrun and anyone managed to get out of it. When they reached one of these, choppers would come in for them. Now all they had to do was to stay ahead of the VC in the area for a couple of hours.

CHAPTER FOUR

Reider took point, followed by Williams. Kosun brought up drag, pushing the stragglers along, giving his Yards a kick in the ass to keep them moving. Most of them wanted to stop and lay some fire down on the camp. It was too late for that to do any good; already the sounds of firing in the camp were less rapid. The last holdouts were being eliminated. Reider was glad the death cry of the camp was muffled by the trees and the patch of thick brush they were moving through.

Reider burst through the brush to find a four-man Viet mortar crew breaking down their piece. He pulled down on them, getting two in the back as they bent over the mortar butt plate, breaking it loose. The others went down as Williams placed two steady shots with his pistol. One round each, in the head. Reider hoped they'd meet no more. They were too close to being in the clear and heading for home.

There was no time for talk and no need. All the men in the escape party knew what the others were thinking: LIM! If they ever got their hands on that son of a bitch, they'd feed him his own guts on a string.

Reider, like Williams, had been in the business too long to let his emotions take complete control. The hate was there, but now it was pushed to the back of his mind. He didn't have time to think about what had happened to the others in their team. They'd bought it. He could only hope that they had gone quickly instead of having the VC take them alive to play with. That was the biggest fear in this kind of war. Not being killed—that was accepted as an occupational hazard. But the thought of being taken alive—of having no control over what was going to be done to you—scared the shit out of the toughest of them. And the VC had little love for the members of the 5th Special Forces Group Vietnam. They took a special pleasure in seeing how much pain they could inflict on any "Beret" they took alive.

They crested a small rocky hill, leading to a

plateau, and looked back. The glow of the burning camp was easily seen over the trees and haze below them. Explosions accented the picture as the remaining fifty-five-gallon drums of diesel and gasoline in the POL went up in geysers of greasy flame.

Reider leaned against a tree, chest heaving from the exertion of breaking through the jungle to this spot. He figured they'd covered four miles. They still had another three miles to go; he was glad that most of it would be through no more than waist-high elephant grass. To the east, the horizon was growing grey with the new dawn. Soon it would be light.

Williams pointed out a small dark shadow in the sky over the camp. An L-19, the Army's version of what a Piper Cub should look like, was checking out the camp. In less than an hour, they knew, gunboats, fighters and bombers would be over what remained of Plei Jrong, and pickup choppers would be heading for each of the rendezvous points to collect any survivors. With a little luck they would be back with the B Team on the hill outside Pleiku in less than two hours.

Lim ducked when an oil drum flew past his head. The Vietnamese members of the Strikers still holding out had given his men more resistance than he'd expected. Another explosion singed the side of his face. He wished he knew who it was that had thrown a white phosphorous grenade and set off the POL dump. His men and those of

the NVA had been given strict orders not to use
incendiaries. The supplies in this camp could keep
a VC battalion equipped for months.

When the Bo Doi captain beside him had been
killed, he'd seen the Montagnards and Americans
making their break, but he'd had no time to waste
on them, nor men to spare. He needed all his
forces to finish off the South Viets still holding out
in one bunker and a trench, and to strip the camp
of arms and munitions, before daylight exposed
him to attack from the air.

He knew from first-hand experience the deadly
effect of American airpower on men caught in the
open. His people would have less than an hour to
complete their mission and reach the protective
canopy of the jungle, before an airstrike could be
made against them.

Lim ordered the VC troops to hold their fire; it
came to a ragged halt as the word was passed
around the camp. The Vietnamese Strikers held
their fire, too, waiting to see what was going to
happen. They knew they were dead men. It was
only a matter of time.

Lim picked his words with care. "Comrades!"
he called to the Strikers, "This must not be.
Brother should not fight brother. It serves no
one's purpose but the Americans and their
puppets in their palaces in Saigon. You know that
the time when we will be ruled by foreigners who
have nothing but contempt for the masses has
come to an end. We will be masters in our own
land, and those who fight for the cause of freedom

will be honored. Those who do not join our cause will be treated in the manner they have merited.

"I have served with you many months in this camp. I know that you are good men who have been led astray by the lies of the imperialists. Lay down your arms and join us, your true brothers, and none shall be harmed. If you refuse this offer, then you will die and the names of your families will be added to our list of the People's enemies. You have five minutes to decide. I pray you will not force me to give the order which will mean your deaths. We are your only hope for the future. Vi dan chien dau! We fight for the people!"

Lim was rather pleased with his speech. It did have a good ring to it. He checked his watch to count off the minutes. It didn't take the full five. In less than three, he heard four quick bursts from Strikers' carbines. With a quick shout he kept his own men from firing. He thought he knew what the shots meant. A handkerchief on the end of a rifle stuck out over the top of a trench. The shots had silenced those who still wished to continue fighting.

Lim called, "Welcome, brothers! Lay down your arms and join us. We welcome you to the struggle for Chien Dau. Liberation is not far away."

The Viet Strikers did as they were ordered, and laid down their weapons to be collected by the VC, then were put to work stripping the camp. Medicines and weapons, even the boots from the dead were taken.

Wounded Strikers were killed without hesitation. Lim had no interest in taking prisoners along who could only slow him down.

Lim looked at the now dimly visible line of hills and regretted that he'd let Williams and Reider get away. Especially Reider. He had never liked him very much. But if the spirits were kind, they would meet again, and he would be able to finish his job. Still, considering everything, the operation was a success. He had taken the camp with acceptable losses and with the new "volunteers" added to his force he had actually increased his strength.

As far as the Americans were concerned, he had killed eight out of the twelve. Mac Rigsby and Sizemore had been safe on their supply run to Pleiku, and Williams and Reider had managed to get away. Still, eight out of twelve was not bad at all. He was pleased with himself. Now to get away. He could hear the thin droning of a small aircraft engine in the distance. It was time to leave behind what had once been the strong point Plei Jrong for the safety of the Cambodian border, only fifteen miles away. Once there the Americans could not follow or harm them. The fools!

Reider's face was a study in controlled anger as the HU-1B helicopter carrying him and Williams flew over what remained of Plei Jrong, followed by three other "Slicks" carrying what was left of the Montagnard Strikers. The camp bore little resemblance to what they had been living in for the last year. When the VC had pulled out, everything had been put to the torch. Not a building was standing, only smoke and flames. They could see bodies on the ground; Americans ran from one body to another searching for any sign of life.

He and Williams had wanted to go back in with the reaction force from Pleiku, but orders had come over the radio for the chopper to bring them back to Pleiku, to give the B Team a briefing on what had happened at the camp. There was nothing they could do at Plei Jrong any more. They were the only survivors. A Mike Force was already on site. If anything could be done, they would do it, and that included any pursuit of the vanished enemy.

The flight back to the red dusty chopper pad at the B Team seemed unreal to Lt. Williams. He held his hands over his eyes, trying to put everything in place in his mind. So much had happened in such a short period of time. It was hard to realize that so many were dead, when they'd been splitting a couple of beers just the night before. Playing cards and telling lies that no one was expected to believe, but all pretended to accept as gospel.

Death somehow always seemed unreal to Williams when it came to people he knew personally. And these deaths he did take very personally. They had been betrayed by a man he'd respected and trusted. Lim had been the one South Vietnamese he'd been absolutely certain of. He'd killed VC in fire fights; even saved the life of Chandler once when they'd been ambushed. Lim had had a hundred opportunities to do them dirt.

It gave Williams a new insight into the minds of the enemy, the patience and dedication it took to spend years as a deep agent waiting for just the right time before showing your true colors. Wearily, he wondered just what Lim had felt. Had he ever really liked any of them? Did he feel the slightest sense of remorse at killing men he'd eaten, drunk and partied with? That was the hard part to accept.

Reider wasn't quite so bewildered. This was his third tour. There had been other camps where South Vietnamese, thought loyal for years, had provided the same service for the Cong. There was a general rule of thumb: you always figured that at least ten percent of your native strike force were either active VC or at least sympathizers, who'd do you in the first chance they got.

To Reider, Lim had always seemed just a little too good, a little too anxious to be a good sport, a little too reliable, always there when you needed something. Never a harsh word from him. Always the completely dedicated soldier against communism.

There was never anything Reider could put his finger on, and Chandler wouldn't have believed him anyway, not after Lim had saved his life. Unless he'd had ironclad proof, which he hadn't. He'd only had a feeling that behind Lim's smooth handsome exterior, was something that was unhealthy.

One day he would pay the son of a bitch back, Reider thought now, even if he had to extend his time in country for another tour. He and the good Captain Lim were not through with each other yet. . . .

CHAPTER FIVE

Mac Rigsby was at the HQ supply building gathering some things for his dispensary back at Plei Jrong, when the word came that the camp had been hit and overrun. He raced to the hut and rolled a red-eyed and half-drunk Sizemore out of the rack, pounding on his ribcage while screaming at him, "Get up! Get UP! They got the camp! Up!"

Once Sizemore managed to focus one bleary eye on the short, barrel-chested Black Irishman and understood what Mac was saying, he sobered up instantly, uncurling his lanky, six-foot, Alabama frame from the floor. It took a few moments for his legs to function properly. Cursing in a constant stream of profanities about every god in the known world, he dragged Mac with him to the commo room, where he threatened the commo man with immediate castration if he didn't get somebody on the set who could tell him what the shit was going on at his camp! Who'd got hit? Who was alive or wounded? How many of the Strike Force survived? When did the attack take place, and how many units were involved? Were they VC or PAVN? Was anyone taken prisoner?

There was no way for the commo man to give him any info other than that two Americans had been picked up in the jungle and were being brought into the SFOB now.

Returning to their hut, Mac and Sizemore threw together their combat kits—weapons, ammo and rations only. A shadow coming in the door interrupted their preparations. It was Major Anderson, the Executive Officer.

"Slow down, Sizemore. There's nothing you can do now. We already have a Mike Force in Plei Jrong. I just finished talking to the team leader. There's not a damned thing you can do, so take your fucking gear off and settle down. Williams and Reider and about twenty Yards are the only survivors." He answered the next questions before Sizemore or Mac could ask them. "It was an inside job. I've talked with Lt. Williams on the chopper radio. It was Lim. He was a mole. And he's gone.

The camps been stripped of everything they could move, and what they didn't take, they burned. He's probably across the border in Cambodia by now, and there's not a damned thing we can do about going after him. So just get control of yourself and wait for Williams and Reider to get in. Then we'll see what the next step will be."

Sizemore and Mac didn't like it, but they knew the Major was right. All they could do was wait for the next few minutes till the Huey touched down. But there was one thing Size wanted, and that was some blood. He was an old-fashioned southern boy who believed in paying his debts, an eye for an eye and maybe the balls too. . . .

When the chopper touched down on the dusty pad to let Williams and Reider off, they were taken immediately to HQ to brief Col. Mendoza, the CO, and Higgins, the Intell Officer. Mac and Sizemore were permitted to sit in the back of the room and listen, provided they kept their mouths shut, which was pretty damned hard for Sizemore to do, but somehow he managed it. Once the briefing was finished, he and Mac left, heading for the hut where they were bunked, to get out Jack Daniels and a bottle of Johnny Walker Red.

Shock, and the first feeling of numbness, was beginning to settle in on Size. He was now the old man of the team, since Vidreen had been wasted. Sizemore had WWII and Korea as well as two previous tours in Nam behind him. Still it was always hard to just accept the fact that so many of his friends had ceased to exist. Maybe it would have been easier for him if he'd been there at the fight. But to hear it like this? He felt guilty somehow about still being alive, unhurt. If he'd been there, things might have turned out different. The thought bothered him, though he knew it was stupid. He'd lost men before, but there was a special feeling to those in the Special Forces. They were closer to him than the others he'd served with over the years. There was a bond between them that he'd never felt in any other unit. They were family, not just teammates. They had been tested and had passed in the toughest school of all. They were Pros.

It was late afternoon before the body bags were brought in from the camp. By this time Williams and Reider had been turned over to Sizemore and Mac, who'd been given direct orders to stay in their quarters. The reunion was not one where songs were sung. Only the cracking of new bottles was heard for some time. There was no need for explanations or any desire to dwell on the deaths of their friends. This was a wake, held in their time-honored fashion. Reider and the rest of them, including Williams, drank themselves into a dull stupor.

Major Anderson, passing by, stopped, then decided it would be best to leave them alone. There was no need for them to see what had been done to their friends. They'd know without being told. In the morning, they'd be in better control of themselves. Still, he wouldn't want to be in the sandals of any VC who fell into their hands for the next

few months. These boys played the game the way
the Viets did when it was necessary, or they had a
score to settle.

Anderson shook his head. Earlier he had watched the bodies of the Americans being loaded into
the back of a deuce and half for the short ride over
to the airfield at Holloway, on the other side of
Pleiku. There they'd be put on a Caribou transport
for the flight to the central graves registration
depot at Ton Son Nhut airfield, outside Saigon.

It was nearly midnight when Captain Murphy,
the Chaplain for the Special Forces in II Corps,
came around to check on the men. He'd just flown
in on a C-130 from Nha Trang, where he'd gotten
the word about Plei Jrong. Murphy was a fighting
man's chaplain. A feisty, grey-templed Irish Catholic who never pushed in where he wasn't wanted,
he had what most priests would have thought unusual priorities. He'd made himself one of the
group when he had had to explain to the Chaplain
General why he'd blown away nine VC at Plei
Tanang Le one night. He'd come in on a chopper
when he heard the camp had been hit to give what
moral support he could to the defenders. During
the course of his attempts to comfort and console
to the wounded, he was attacked by the Cong.
"Sir," he said to the Chaplain General, "there's a
time for fighting and those sons o' bitches were
shooting at me!" He probably would have been
sent stateside if he hadn't been the only chaplain
around that the Special Forces men accepted as
one of them.

When he went in Mac and Size's room, he nearly choked from the cigarette smoke and whiskey fumes. They were just sitting around, with glazed expressions on their faces, sucking on the whiskey, saying nothing. Murphy held out the bottle he had brought. Mac took it, cracked the top and slid his butt over a bit to make room for him on the bunk. Murphy took a long pull of the bourbon, tucking his knees up under his chin. As the bottles were passed around, he took his turn each time. These men had their own way of getting rid of their grief.

Nothing was said that night as they drank themselves unconscious, but they all somehow felt better that Murphy had shown up. Even Sizemore, who professed to be a devout atheist and religiously avoided churches.

When they rolled out in the morning, there was no need to dwell on what had happened any further. The dead were already on their way back home, as if that made any difference to them. Now it was for the living to do their jobs.

Once Williams got his eyes open, he found a fresh clean uniform outside his door. The supply sergeant was on the ball. After showering and shaving he presented himself to Col. Mendoza.

"Sit down Williams!" The colonel indicated a rattan chair, made locally.

Williams did as he said, a bit queasy from the night before.

Mendoza sent for coffee and waited till Williams had taken a couple of swallows before continuing.

"I don't have to tell you the way we all feel. I've gone through this several times now. The last three camps that have been overrun were all taken with inside help, but this is the first time it's been someone like Lim. You know, we've kicked the shit out of them pretty good for the last few months. They must have decided they needed a win pretty bad to blow his cover. He was on the way up and scheduled for promotion. We'll probably never catch up to him, but we're going to try. He's marked now, and the word has been sent out that whoever can put us onto him will be paid enough gold out of the Head Money fund to retire on."

Mendoza poured a cup of coffee for himself, lacing it with a touch of Jack Daniels. He offered some to Williams, whose stomach did a half turn as he refused. "No, thanks. What about us, sir? Where do we go now?" When something like this happened, the survivors of a team were usually broken up and sent out as replacements to other camps who'd lost men with their MOS.

"I know what you're thinking, but not this time. I've got something else for you and your people to do. I want you to start up a new Mike Force company using your surviving Yards and Noncoms as the nucleus.

That appealed to Williams; he smiled.

Colonel Mendoza poured another coffee for himself. "I want you to stay up here and work. You know the area, and I want to have a reaction team that's ready to move on an instant's notice. One that I can depend on. I want you to use only Yards

who, like your own people, have lost friends and
family to Charley. I don't want to take any chances
of having infiltrators in your unit. If you find one,
or suspect anyone strong enough, I'll leave it to
your judgment as how best to deal with him."

Williams knew what he meant. The slang phrase
for that kind of judgment was "terminate with extreme prejudice." One of those weird terms the
military had such a propensity for. They couldn't
just say "kill the mother" and let it go at that.

Mendoza concluded, "You can go tell your people what's coming down. I want you all to take a
week's R&R in Nha Trang. That'll give me time to
set things in motion. You can pick them up this
afternoon. I'll have my Intell Officer divert some
Head Money so you can all have some bucks in
your pockets. When you get back, we'll talk about
missions. I have a couple of things coming up. But
first I want to make certain all the crap is cleared
out from between your men's ears before putting
them back to work."

Nha Trang was one of the most beautiful beach
areas in Nam. A busy city that had been left pretty
much alone by the war, it was valuable to the Cong
as a source of supplies and money. An occasional
mortar round or two missed the airfield and blew
away a couple of horses now and then. But, for the
most part, it was a resort area for the men on the
Fifth Special Forces Group and the other military
units stationed there. Here they could lie around
for a time, eyeball the roundeyed nurses, and then
head for the club Nautique or the New York Bar,

where pretty Vietnamese hostesses in miniskirts or the more attractive, light, flowing ao dais would hustle them for drinks.

Nha Trang was the Headquarters for all Special Forces teams in Nam, and most of the men at HQ spent their time trying to get out of it and into the field. Here they were too much under the eye of the regular Army as represented by MACV, the Military Assistance Command Vietnam.

Their first order of business when the C-130 touched down was to drop their gear at the SF Transient Barracks and shower, head for the Club Nautique, then take a cab to François' down the coast about ten clicks. It was one of the safe restaurants in the area; its customers were never attacked coming or going by Charley. They knew that owners paid off the Cong for that privilege, but who the hell wanted to make waves? Francois' had lobster so big it took four grown men to consume one, and crayfish the size of regular lobsters. In the old days, four men could get fed for five or six dollars but now, since the buildup, those the Special Forces considered tourists had driven the prices up by overpaying on everything from Bamiba beer to pussy. But Francois' still beat the shit out of the flytraps in Pleiku.

When they touched down, Williams was called to HQ and given his orders promoting him to captain. He didn't know whether it was because he'd earned it, or whether it was a bonus for surviving Plei Jrong. Whichever, it meant a few more dollars in his pocket and more control over the fate of his men; that was the most important thing about it.

He found Sizemore and the rest of his crew gathered around a table at the Nautique, doing their best to pickle their brains with formaldehyde-laced Bamiba and Beer Larue chased with straight shots of Jim Beam. When the rest of the whiskies ran low in Nam, it seemed there was always some Beam to be had.

Sizemore rolled one red-rimmed eye at Williams when he came in out of the bright sunlight. Williams was picture perfect in new, clean, pressed and starched jungle fatigues. Size rolled his bloodshot eyes up to the top of his head when he saw the new captain bars on William's collar tabs.

"Oh, my God, men!" He addressed the rest of the crew, drawing their attention to this bright and shining apparition that had come to them out of the sun. "I do believe we have an 'Ossifer' type captain watching us!"

He held a finger to his nose in a conspiratorial manner and whispered, "Shhhh! Maybe it will go away if we ignore it."

Williams shoved him over, pulling a chair up to the table. He took one of Mac's beers away from him, downing it in one swallow, letting the cold fluid flow straight down his throat. The cold brew hit his gut, immediately causing a sharp piercing pain between his eyes. He waited a second for it to pass before responding to Sizemore's jibes.

"Enjoy yourselves, animals! In a few days you'll be working your asses off, and while you're at it, get off mine, or I'll tell the local medics that your shot records were lost in the camp." The threat of having to take all their shots over again, especially the gamma globulin, which was administered according to body weight, brought an abrupt change to the team's manner of addressing their new captain. While their fearless leader was talking to Reider about what he would need in the way of supplies when they went back to Pleiku, Sizemore hurriedly whispered in Mac's ear, who nodded his head in agreement, then gave a spontaneous giggle that he couldn't control. Williams looked at them suspiciously but only saw two happy, sweaty, smiling, faces beaming at him.

The next morning, Williams found out what Size and Mac had been smiling about. He received a call from the SF Surgeon to report to the dispensary. When he got there, he saw a familiar array of hypodermics loaded with everything from cholera vaccine to plague.

Jenkins, the surgeon, grinned evilly. "I heard you lost your shot records. In that case, you'll have to take the whole series over again. Sorry about that." He didn't sound very sorry to Williams.

If Williams was going to have his arms and ass perforated by multiple wounds, he wouldn't be the only one to suffer. "What about the rest of my team Doc? They'll need their shots too."

Jenkins leered as if Williams were a hot piece of young tender meat. He really enjoyed giving shots to the SF troopers. It tickled him that so many of the big tough, parachuting, ranger-qualified heros had such a fear of his needles. It made him feel almost . . . godlike. "I know that. They should be here any moment."

He was right on cue; the screen door slammed to announce the presence of Williams' team. Jenkins gave them the same grin he'd given their commander, but it didn't seem to have the same effect.

Size, Mac and Reider, grinning from ear to ear, all pulled clean, neat copies of their personal shot records from their billfolds. Every shot was up to date and signed.

Williams opened his mouth to protest, but closed it again. There was nothing he could do but grit his teeth. Mac must have used his influence among his medic friends to get bogus shot records for the others. Tears leaked from Williams' eyes as the thick needle, used to administer the gamma globulin, penetrated the fleshy meat of his buttock. Silently, between groans, he swore vengeance on the traitors as they enjoyed his misery.

It was late afternoon when they all met at the Nautique. Williams' eyes opened wide when Size came in wearing dirty blue bikini trunks. The front of his body from nose to toes, was a mass of thick scabs and abrasions; he was picking small pieces of gravel out of his skin, cursing everybody and everything in this lousy country. Sizemore was a bit reluctant to explain what had happened, but after a couple of straight shots he 'fessed up.

"I was minding my own damned business, coming up from the beach just a few minutes ago. I flagged down a cyclo cab and was sitting in the back of it relaxing, enjoying the ride here, when out of the shadows of an alley I saw this thing come flying through the air right into the cab with me. Naturally, I did the only logical thing. I screamed grenade and threw myself out of the seat, hitting the ground face first, scrambling to get some fucking distance between me and the cyclo. That's where I got the gravel burns."

Mac prodded him. "What about the grenade?"

Size looked indignant. "That's what pisses me off. It wasn't a grenade! Some damned kid about five years old tossed a beercan at me. If I could have caught the little bastard, I'd have grabbed him by both legs, tossed him in the air and made a wish!"

Size permitted a waitress to bring over some damp towels to clean the worst of the dirt from his tender front. He'd be sore for days, and with the way his knees felt, if he was going to get any ass the girl would have to do all the work.

Williams sat on the edge of his chair trying to control a fit of laughter. The gods were kind! Already he had been paid back a bit on his debt. He knew that he didn't have to do a damn thing directly to punish them. They were more than capable of doing it to themselves without his help. He was very, very pleased with the manner in which fate had taken a hand in his vengeance.

Size sucked down three iced Bamibas to help ease the tender portions of his anatomy.

Williams noticed Reider hadn't been in on the general laughter at Sizemore's plight and recalled that he had kept a sullen look on his face all day. That bothered him. "What is it? You might as well get it off your chest."

Reider wiped a hand across his forehead. Even under the fans, the June humidity on the coast brought beads of sweat to every face. "It's Lim, sir. I want his ass and I want it bad."

Williams knew how he felt, but he couldn't let that influence their new assignment—not yet, anyway. "I feel the same way you do. Remember, I was there too. But I won't put up with any bullshit that I don't authorize. So knock if off or get out of the team. I don't want to have someone out there that I have to worry about. We can't afford a vendetta right now. If things work out right, and we can get some control over our assignments, we'll put out the word among the Montagnard tribes to watch for him. And that is all we can do at this point. So just shape up!"

Reider knew he was right. Still it didn't make things any easier. He knew the rest of them wanted Lim's ass as badly as he did. If there was any way they could get a line on the son of a bitch, they'd go after him, no matter what HQ might say about it. They had a history of taking care of their own, and MACV could go fuck themselves if they didn't like it. What were they going to do? Send them to Vietnam?

A bellowing came from the street door as a massive shadow blocked out the sunlight. A roar for whiskeys drowned out the jukebox and all attempts at conversation. Once inside, the huge form of Jay Marshall, all six foot six of him, wearing khaki bermudas, a sick purple-flowered hawaiian shirt, and a maroon beret, made his presence known. Once Marshall's eyes focused, and he saw Reider and the others, he made for them, ignoring the protests of those at the tables he knocked over in moving through the room. He was not a very graceful creature at the best of times, and when he had a skinful, which was most of the time, he had all the agility of a bull water buffalo in heat.

"Reider!" he bellowed. The vocal projection he was capable of would have made Caruso green with envy. It was commonly rumored that Big Jay had learned to whisper in a steel mill.

Reider cringed. He knew what was coming next, and braced himself for it as best he could be grabbing the seat of his chair with both hands and holding on.

It didn't do any good. One of Jay's paws brushed Reider's shoulder in a friendly pat that knocked him off his chair and over into the next table, ruining a F-15 pilot's tale of glory to a bored bar girl sipping her Saigon tea and wondering whether to take a chance on slipping the flyboy a Mickey just to shut him up.

Jay roared out, "Wine for my men! We've been raping and ravaging since dawn, and we thirst, you swine!" A Chinese waitress, familiar with his histrionics, brought over two fifths of Jack Daniels, ignoring his paw reaching up her genuine imitation silk cheongsam. Jay blustered a lot, but he was the softest touch around for every sob story and implausible lie that could be told, and was always good for at least a fifty-dollar tip in green money rather than script or piastres. Air America paid very well indeed.

He greeted everyone profusely, and reached across the table to shake Mac's hand; Mac held up Jay's index finger. It was the size of a Hormel hotdog. Mac examined the hairy hand carefully, then said to Jay in dead serious tones, "You know, Jay, if you'd shave your hand regular for a while and let a really good pelt of hair grow on it, I might be able to get you some stud fees for it as a German shepherd."

Jay thoughtfully screwed up the sagebrush that served as his eyebrows, then shook his head. "I ain't got time right now, but I'll keep it in mind for when the shit over here ends and I'm out of work."

Jay spotted the new rank insignia on Williams' collar. He was amazed and pleased; Williams' promotion gave him an excuse to buy rounds for the house. He turned serious for just one second. "I'm sorry to hear about the guys in your camp. They were a good bunch; I liked working with them. If there's anything I can do to help find that cocksucker, what's his name? Just call any time. . . ." That was it. The sadness had been spoken out loud, and it was done with. Gone to the past where it belonged.

Most of Williams' team had gotten in pretty tight with the CIA spooks over the years, having done more than one piece of dirty work for them. They were especially tight with the ones who had to fly them in and out of operations, like Jay, who was both chopper and fixed-wing qualified, with thousands of hours in each. They were the crazy men of Air America—the flying mercenaries of the CIA's personal airline, who flew everything from ammo to pigs in and out of nearly every country in the world. It was they who'd kept the fight going against the Pathet Lao for the last six years by flying ammo, food and agents into the highlands, where the Meo tribesmen operated against the Ho Chi Minh trail and Pathet Lao Viet outposts; tying up thousands of the enemy to guard the trails in from the north.

Reider had been on two operations for the Company while in country. Both of them had been in Laos, where they'd based out of the secret camp the CIA had built in the mountains. It was from Long Tieng that special teams were sent out to harass, ambush, and in some cases, remove a particular individual.

The second operation had begun just three months ago, when he and Kosun had been hauled out of the rack to board a C-46 at five in the morning along with one platoon of Montagnard Stikers. Montagnards were preferred for clandestine operations outside South Vietnam for a couple of reasons. They were more reliable then Viets where loyalty was concerned, and if any of them were killed and the bodies left behind, no one could distinguish them from any of the other hill tribesmen of Laos and Cambodia. If an American was killed, and the survivors couldn't bury the body, orders were to burn it or blow it up so no positive identification could be made. The North Viets and Pathet Lao loved to scream to the UN that their borders had been violated. . . .

"Three months ago. . . . God!" Reider thought. "It seems like twenty years. Maybe thirty-four is too old for this kind of work?"

CHAPTER SIX

The next five days were spent partying and mooching the things they would need when they returned to the highlands to set up their Mike Force. Reider bought three bottles of Jim Beam for Kosun; that should keep the old barbarian off his ass for two or three days.

Their last night before leaving the decadent pleasures of Nha Trang for the central highlands was spent with Jay, who picked up the tab on everything. They'd started early because Williams

wanted everyone bright-eyed, or at least able to
focus when they boarded the plane next morning
at 0600 hours.

It wasn't a very drunk evening, for a change.
After five days around the huge base, with its hundreds of resident petty field marshals and Saigon
commandoes, they were ready to go back to what
they sometimes strangely enough thought of as
home. It was where they belonged. Here every
goddamned thing was politics of one form or
another. Every swinging dick was shuffling for
points. The few good units that had the misfortune
of being permanently based in Nha Trang spent
most of their time trying to get out of it.

That evening at the Nautique, Williams and
Sizemore pulled over into a corner, where they
were raking a fighter pilot's ass over the coals. The
pilot had been in country two months and was
running his mouth, saying how much he enjoyed
dropping napalm, and he didn't give a shit who he
laid it on. All gooks were the same. Then he related
some tired old story of children with hand grenades, and booby-trapped baby buggies.

Sizemore had pinned his ass to the table, and
since Williams had the same rank as the pilot, the
conversation was conducted on equal terms. Sizemore smiled at the pilot, his words softened by his
slight southern accent but his intent deadly: "So.
You like dropping jellied gasoline and don't care
where it lands? Kill all the gooks! Men, women
and children. No matter where they are? Let me
tell you something, sonny. If that's the way we're

going to run this damn war, then we deserve to lose. It's thinking like that which has set us back years in this country. You drop one bomb of napalm on a friendly village and you'll have a thousand volunteers joining the VC ranks, that we'll have to face with guns in their hands. I only hope you have that same privilege one day. I know your job is tough, but you don't see the people you're killing, and you don't see your own dead. If you're here long enough, maybe you'll learn something about soldiering. And I'll tell you this, with my captain sitting here. I might work over an enemy soldier who has information, which might save the lives of some of my people, because he'd do the same to me. But if my commander ever gave me orders to waste a child, or wipe out some unarmed civilians, then I'd probably put him away."

The young pilot tried to interrupt Sizemore's tirade, but was stopped by a firm hand on his shoulder pinning him to his chair as Williams told him, "Just sit there and listen."

Sizemore caught his second wind. "If we obey orders like that, then there should never have been no Nuremburg trials for war criminals, because there'd be no difference between us and the Nazis, or the Japs in World War Two, and I was there. They all said they were only following orders, and that's a bunch of shit. In our army, an order like that is unlawful, and no one, regardless of rank, has to obey it. I'm a soldier, not a baby butcher, and if you don't like it, young sir, then you are certainly welcome to haul your ass off that chair and make anything of it you choose to. Because I am sick of listening to you fucking amateurs!"

Williams said, "Take it easy, Sarge. He's still an officer."

The pilot looked relieved and pleased at Williams' interjection, and the recognition of his inherent superiority, but Williams poked a hole in his bubble. "No, Sergeant, you can't offer to take a captain's head off. But I can!" He pointed a finger under the now alarmed sky jockey's nose, then pointed at Sizemore, then himself. "What he said, son of a bitch! I think you better go back to school or talk to some of the pilots who've been over here a while before you start running your mouth again."

The fighter pilot beat a hasty retreat from the club. He was still not sure what he had said that was wrong, but there was no way he was going to argue with those crazy bastards. You'd think they liked the Gooks or something.

Williams brought Size back over to the table and Reider, Mac and Jay, saying, "I wonder how gung ho he'd be if he'd been fighting for thirty years with no end in sight and nothing but greedy fucking politicians ripping you off every chance they get? If the spooks would snuff out the politicos, theirs and ours, we'd be able to handle the countryside with no problem. But till something is done, we just do the best we can, because the thieving bastards in Saigon are still better to have around than the commies." Williams got up, not finishing his drink. "I'm packing it in. I don't feel much like partying now. You guys just don't get in any trouble, and be on the flight line by 0530."

He was followed by Size. Then Mac and Reider said goodbye to Jay, with the promise to tie on a good one in Singapore or Hong Kong when they got their next R&R.

Jay watched them leave, thinking: Those are some damn good people. Too bad so many of them are going to die. But the good always get it first. Maybe it's because they care?

He left his bottle on the table and got up. The desire to drink had gone out the door with them. He suddenly had a bitter taste in his mouth. He'd be glad to get back in the sky where he belonged. He'd had enough of the real world.

The sun was already heating up the flight line when they crawled in the open tailgate and found places on the canvas seats to strap in. Their gear was stowed by the cargo master up forward. Once they were airborne and clear of the ridge of mountains surrounding Nha Trang, Reider and Mac lay down on a pile of cargo chutes to catch up on their sleep, while the others just slumped over, heads against their chests, to wait it out until they heard the grinding hydraulics putting down the landing gear for their approach to Holloway and Pleiku.

When the tailgate opened, the first face they saw was that of Kosun. How had he known when they'd be coming in? As usual, he wasn't going to tell them anything he didn't have to. Still, it was good to see a familiar face. They checked back into

the Special Forces compound, and Williams went
for his briefing with Maj. Anderson. By the time he
got back, Sizemore and the others were out in-
specting the new bodies Kosun had recruited for
them. Most were natives from nearby villages.
Only a few had any combat experience and most of
those were the survivors of Plei Jrong. Since
Reider was the light weapons man, most of their
initial training would come under his supervision,
though all the others would pitch in where needed,
especially Sizemore, who was cross-trained in
everybody's job.

Kosun's knowledge of Montagnard dialects was,
as usual, invaluable. He seemed to know everything from Bihnar to Mnong, besides having a fair
grasp of German and naturally his French, but he
still refused to speak any more English than was
absolutely necessary. Reider, who knew him best,
just figured that he didn't like the feel of English.
He had long since given up trying to make Kosun
do anything he didn't want to.

For a month they ran the recruits through their
own form of basic training, with special attention
paid to ambushes, both setting them up and being
caught in them. Like most of the natives in the
highlands, the Yards had to be taught by example.
It was a giant step from their homemade crossbow
or hunting spear to light machineguns, mortars
and grenade launchers. At first, the only discipline
they accepted was from Kosun. To them he was
the elder, and as they didn't know what tribe he
was from, he was best suited to settling arguments

among them. The Americans they obeyed out of fear and respect. They feared them because they were unknown and unpredictable. The Duum Brunn—bignoses—were not like the Vietnamese, or any other men they'd seen before. They respected them because these strangers ate with them, slept with them, and all wore brass or copper tribal bracelets, showing they had been adopted into the tribes and were worthy of respect.

Williams and Sizemore spent most of their time trying to set up a new intelligence network among the nonaligned tribes of the region, while Mac did his best to train some medics, using a mixture of penicillin and witchcraft to impress his students.

The Yards were mostly animists who believed in the spirits of the fields and streams. To them, medicine had to have some kind of ceremony attached to it or else it wouldn't work very well. Mac invented several rites—one of his favorites was the singing of "Hey, bobba reeba" when giving a shot —in order to prevent them from using their own magic, such as packing an open wound in cow dung or tying eggs on the wrists of people with malaria so that the egg would soak up the fever.

No one's job was easy, but the Special Forces liked the Montagnards and understood them better than anyone else in Nam. These Yards were the personal property of the Mike Force Group, and were watched over as a mother watches over her child.

Once their initial basic training was over and

Reider was reasonably sure they wouldn't blow off their own feet, it was time to take them out, one platoon at a time, on a short search-and-destroy mission. Reider always picked areas that were normally free of VC activity for such missions. He didn't want the Yards in a hard firefight before they were ready. It was best to let them get a couple of easy kills in first. As always, they'd learn a lot faster by doing, than by being told.

He checked around with the other camps to see what was happening in their areas. Most of the camps kept a couple of spots staked out where Charley kept rice stored. They used these the same way Reider wanted to. If a new man came in, they'd take him to one of these sites and sit down and wait. In time, one or more VC would come by for some rice; then their new man could get his cherry kill in and lose any buck fever he might have had, with little danger to himself or the men with him. Of course, they didn't tell him it was a cherry site until he had been on a couple more operations. It was important for him to think he had done it all by himself.

Reider was planning to take the whole company out for two days in the field, but Size culled out the veterans for a backup force. They'd had word that Plei Me, to the southeast of Pleiku, might get hit; the CO wanted some experienced men available just in case. Reider was given one platoon of recruits, with Kosun as native commander and interpreter.

Sizemore watched them board the choppers for

the ride out and wished them well. He knew that Reider and Kosun could take care of themselves, but with new men you never knew . . . . He liked Reider. The grey-eyed, stocky soldier was a good solid type, who did his job and never bitched about it too much. He was a good steady soldier you could depend on. The chopper banked and turned west to fly above highway 19 leading to the border with Cambodia. They'd set down some ten miles this side of it and set up a watch on a known trail for VC infiltrators. With luck, they might be able to ambush a small group coming in off the Ho Chi Minh trail.

CHAPTER SEVEN

Reider could feel the rivulets of sweat running down the matted hairs of his chest and soaking the back of his uniform, gluing him to the rough bark of the tree at his back. The night sounds of the jungle grated on his ears. He sat motionless in the underbrush, tense, ears straining for that unnatural sound that meant Charley, the M-3 submachinegun cradled across his knees.

He waited for the first red glow of dawn.

He'd always hated this time before the morning,

when the night seemed blackest and the heat of
the jungle was at its worst, this time when the
darkness imprisoned him like an animal caged in
the underbrush.

Hot.

He waited. . . .

Slowly, sullenly, like a corpse rising from the
black grave of the dead night, the sky lightened
through the leaves and branches of the trees
overhead, and the birds awakened. The underbrush came alive. A thin mist from the swamps
formed, hanging ghost-low among the trees.

When it was light enough, he checked his men.
They were spread out in the underbrush, hidden
from all sides and from the sky, their tiger-striped
camouflage blending with the trees and grass.
Men from the hill tribes. Short, brown, tough men
in whom the savage was thinly buried. They rested
with their rifles clutched to them like spears as
they also waited for the light of dawn.

Twenty yards away, Kosun also watched the
clearing, his eyes those of a snake, dead inside,
two beads of coldness. Nothing moved. Satisfied,
he moved carefully back through the underbrush
to Reider and touched the light-haired man on the
shoulder.

"Trung Si Mike, nous allons?"

"No, Kosun. We stay put for a minute. I thought
I saw something move over there a few minutes
ago."

"Pas de Cong, Trung Si." Kosun's voice had an
insistent quality to it.

"Quiet, damn it. I don't care if you can't see any-one. We wait. Je reste, goddamn it!" Kosun's refusal to speak English could be irritating at times; Reider's French was barely adequate, despite the best efforts of the instructors at the language school.

Reider turned his gray eyes on the Yard commander and wondered for perhaps the thousandth time about this small, dark man, this crow of a bird with the eyes of a snake and the two swift hands. He was an oldtimer. Kosun himself didn't know his age; he could have been anything from thirty to fifty. But Reider did know that Kosun had more than once saved his life: once in a swamp alive with VC, once on a mountainside when the mortars were whining and shattering the air with red-hot shrapnel. He'd been hit in the legs by the splinters, one of them fractured his left leg below the knee.

Kosun had found him and carried him out on his back over twenty miles to the SF camp, where a chopper came in and took him out to the 8th Field Hospital in Nha Trang. Later, in the States, when he was recovering, and wondering about it, he thought of Kosun often.

Now he was back again, with Kosun as the Yard commander, on another mission, this time with a company of green half-trained recruits. Kosun was impatient, waving toward the clearing. They were too anxious, these Montagnards. Too damned anxious to die. They had a proper Oriental disregard for human life. But Kosun should

know better; he'd been around long enough.
Maybe he was getting to old for this bullshit too!

Kosun crawled twenty yards across the clearing
and started to sweep the treeline again with his
eyes. Nothing moved.

One good thing about the Yards, thought Reider,
they're loyal. He still remembered the time back
at the base when Rogers' patrol had been smeared.
The Yards called him on the radio to say they were
surrounded and Rogers had been hit. That was the
last anyone heard for three hours. When the helicopters found them, the Yards were laid in a circle
around the sergeant. Rather than leave him, they
had all died. The VC had disemboweled him and
filled the cavity in his stomach with red hot coals
while he was still alive.

The Yard detachment had not taken any prisoners for four months after that.

Kosun wriggled through the underbrush toward
him. "Restons-nous ici?"

"Yes, we wait, Kosun. The choppers reported
VC over there. They may still be there for all we
know. Play it cool and stay alive. What are the
broads going to think if you get snuffed before
Saturday?"

Kosun grinned, saying one of the few English
phrases he ever used: "Never happen, GI."

An hour later, Reider watched the Huey skate
over the treetops and away. It was time to do
something. If there'd been any Cong spotted, it
would have let him know. Reider looked across
the clearing and made up his mind. "Okay, I guess

we'll just have to find out the hard way. . . . You hold your people back until I get across the clearing. Then you follow, and for Christ's sake, Kosun, keep 'em spread out!"

Kosun broke in, using a mixture of French and Vietnamese interspersed with American swear words to make his point that he was the commander of the Strikers, and it was his job to take the lead every now and then.

"This is no time for politics, Kosun, damn it."

Kosun said nothing, only looked him straight in the face. Reider searched Kosun's eyes. It was one of the few times Kosun had ever looked human above the nose. The Oriental "face" was at stake. Reider smiled.

"Okay, Kosun, you go first."

"Merci, mon ami."

The American slapped the hill tribesman on the shoulder, and Kosun grinned, showing yellow teeth filed down. He looked once more across the field and moved out, turning in a zigzag, hunched low, his body almost double. In a few seconds he disappeared into the trees on the other side of the clearing.

Reider waited with the remainder of the patrol until Kosun waved to him from the trees, and then they moved forward. The Yard troops started across the clearing upright, their rifles slung on their shoulders.

"Get down!" Reider yelled.

The Montagnards ignored his command.

"Jesus Christ!" Reider screamed. "You cross

open terrain in relays and low! Get those god-
damned weapons off your shoulders! Kosun! Will
you tell these ragged-ass barbarians to spread out
and get down?''

Reider caught a glimpse of Kosun in the trees.
He was doubled over with laughter at Reider's
attempts to communicate. After a few seconds,
Kosun yelled, ''No need, Trung-Si. No need. VC all
gone!''

Silence. Unnatural silence. As though the jungle
were frozen in time.

Then one hell of an explosion as the falling
mortar shells from Charley hit. The rattle of
machineguns. Reider saw the astonishment on
Kosun's face. All the Montagnards were yelling.
Smoke filled the trees and obscured the green
with gray and white clouds. Flashes of light flickered like Christmas lights from the trees.

Reider dropped to one knee and cut loose at the
trees with a long burst. ''Jesus God!'' he yelled.
''Down!'' He made hand motions to emphasize the
meaning.

The Strikers were not waiting for Kosun's translation. They began to spread out and unslung their
weapons. Ragged firing from the patrol started to
hit into the trees. Reider fired two more short
bursts into the trees and looked around for Kosun.
Behind him the 60- and 81mm mortars were falling. Arms and legs were blown into the air, and
bodies dripping red splattered into the spongy
earth. Two men behind him were screaming for a
medic. One had his leg doubled under hm, only a

thin shred of fabric holding it to the hip. Another's face was a mask of hamburger from shrapnel.

"Sergent, Je suis blessé—I'm wounded." The cry was faint.

"Kosun?"

"Sergent Mike! Bac-si. Bac-si."

Reider looked around and saw Kosun crawling toward him from the line of trees. He was calling weakly for a medic. "Bac-si! Bac-si!"

Kosun stopped calling and rolled over, clutching his stomach. A large loop of gut bulged from between his bloody fingers.

Reider began to crawl toward him, firing at the trees as he moved. He heard the whine of slugs and the sound they made as they struck the soft ground. The VC were still gutting the clearing with mortars as well as with machinegun fire. Reider reached Kosun and grabbed him by the wrists.

"Bac-si, Sergent Mike, bac-si."

"Don't sweat, Kosun. We'll get a medic."

Half of Kosun's guts were lying over his belt. There was no use thinking about a medic. The large intestine was a slimy, wet thing, bulging over Kosun's thumbs as he convulsively tried to keep the wound closed. Each time Reider dragged him by the wrists, the torn flesh parted more, and Kosun screamed. The mud was stained red. They made it back ten feet and were pinned down by heavy machinegun fire. Reider dragged Kosun toward the bodies of the Yard troops for protection. Slugs were thumping into the corpses.

It was then that Reider noticed that he was the only one firing at the trees. Of the Yards scattered around the clearing, a few were moving feebly, but the rest were dead. Screams of "Bac-si!" could be heard above the firing from the trees.

Reider fired another burst in the general direction of the machineguns and tried to pull Kosun with one hand. The last thing he remembered was a shriek of the mortar that was much too close and Kosun weakly screaming for a medic. . . .

Silence enveloped the clearing and the surrounding jungle as a dozen small, dark men in black pajamas and ragged uniforms emerged from the underbrush and moved forward slowly. They advanced across the clearing cautiously, with rifles front and bayonets fixed. A few brandished machetes. They stopped at each wounded Montagnard to pierce the skull with bayonets. Then they stripped each body of clothing, ammunition, and personal effects. A number of VC squatted down to replace their own crude, hand-fashioned sandals and rubber-sole shoes with U.S. Army BATA boots.

Reider became aware of sound very slowly—the distant chattering of the VC. He felt himself being rolled off Kosun. Kosun's wound still oozed, and some of the blood was smeared on Reider's face. He rolled to one side heavily and opened his eyes. Kosun moaned, "Bac-si."

"You may as well not fake it, Sergeant," said a quiet voice above and behind him.

Reider blinked at a pair of boots, and then his eyes rose to the face of a North Vietnamese officer. Staring in disbelief, he gathered himself to rise, but someone grabbed him by the hair and jerked his head back down into the dirt with such force he thought his neck had snapped.

"Give me your full attention, Sergeant. I am eager to learn what brings the Special Forces out so early this morning. I must say, you do not look very special right now, however. Your face is filthy, and there is mud in the cut on your head."

The officer laughed derisively. "Perhaps I should observe proper military courtesy. Do you think I should do that, Sergeant?"

Reider did not reply. The voice above him was all to familiar. Bile rose to the back of his throat.

The voice droned on insultingly: "Allow me to introduce myself, Sergeant. I am Major Lim of the Vietnamese People's Army of Liberation. Turn him over," he barked.

Reider was jerked over to his back, his face partially covered by dirt and blood. The major placed one foot on Reider's nameplate and wiped his boot on the mud-stained fatigue shirt.

Reider remained silent, his mind stunned.

A smile began at the corners of Major Lim's mouth and then vanished. "Your uniform is not clean, Sergeant. I cannot see your name for the dirt. Tell it to me."

Reider refused to reply.

A VC infantryman behind him spoke rapidly to Major Lim. Lim replied in like fashion to the foot soldier, and then he addressed himself to Reider. "Well, Sergeant, it seems one of my men wants your boots. You would not object, would you? Big American ranger like you. Why would you have further need of your boots for walks in the jungle?" Lim laughed nastily.

Reider felt small hands seize his legs roughly from behind. His boots were wrenched from his feet as two more VC infantrymen grabbed Reider's jacket, jerked and pulled it from his body, and gave it to Major Lim.

"Reider," Lim spoke distinctly, triumphantly. "Who says there's no such thing as luck? I've thought about you since last we met. Have you thought of me also, Sergeant? I am sure that we have much to talk about. Especially all our old friends at Plei Jrong."

Kosun stirred slightly, murmuring, "Bac-si, Bac-si." A bubbly crimson froth appeared at his lips.

"Your Montagnard friend," Lim began, "I should say, animal, wants a medic. I forget if you have been cross-trained as one or not. Are you a medic, Sergeant? Never mind. Montagnards are useless. But I will give him medicine." Major Lim motioned to one of the waiting Viet Cong. "Sat Moi," he said.

"You bastard," said Reider.

"Silence, Sergeant," said Lim. "I have instructed my men to kill the animal, and there will be no interference from you." Lim signaled his subordinates. "Now!"

One of the VC moved over to Kosun, who lay moaning softly, still whispering, "Bac-si, Bac-si." The VC, at the signal from Lim, pushed the bayonet into Kosun's open mouth until the blade exited from the back of Kosun's skull. Kosun's body trembled and his drumming heels sent up little clouds of red dust.

Reider screamed, berserk with fury.

Another VC placed a bayonet to Reider's throat. Reider felt the point of the blade penetrate, and he choked. Lim stood above him with his hand raised, ready to order the bayonet thrust deeper.

"I ordered you to be silent, Sergeant," said Lim. "Surely you can learn from the fate of your late Montagnard friend that it is not wise to open your mouth. Perhaps I will have my man push the bayonet in more deeply—say a centimeter each second until you scream for him to complete his plunge?"

"Ong Moi," said Reider. "Ong Moi."

"I know you speak a little Vietnamese, Sergeant. But then you Americans have all those fine schools to teach you. Whether I am the Moi, or your now deceased Montagnard, we shall see. I am sure you have some idea in your mind concerning the Geneva Convention. You foreign dogs always demand that we remember, but it is you, Sergeant, who must remember this: I have never lived in Switzerland, and it is a long way from Geneva to Hanoi. You will come to understand that."

Lim motioned to two more VC, who marched with their machetes into the trees and returned moments later with a bamboo pole a little over six feet in length. They pulled Reider's arms behind his back, shoved the pole through his crooked arms underneath the shoulder blades, and lashed his wrists to the pole. Lim gestured to another soldier, who twisted a rope around Reider's neck and gave the end of the rope ceremoniously to Lim. Then Reider was jerked to his feet. The sudden movement started his head pounding again, and the pole behind his back made his movements jerky and uncoordinated. Lim watched the painful way in which Reider steadied himself, and then jerked on the rope. Reider fell to his knees. Because he could no longer maintain his balance, he fell across the butchered body of Kosun. Lim laughed, then pulled hard on the rope and jerked Reider to his feet.

"Sergeant," said Lim, "the only reason your head is not now sticking on a stake with your testicles in your mouth is that later we are going to have a long, long talk. I am sure there is much you will want to tell me. But excuse me for a moment. You seem to have fallen again. Get up."

Reider felt the rope grow taut and tried to move as quickly as possible to avoid the jerk. He gagged again, but gained his feet. They began to move. The entire VC unit, Lim and Reider in the head, crossed the clearing, away from the motionless bodies of the slain Montagnards, into the trees. Lim held to the rope, jerking Reider occasionally, at times pulling him so he wouldn't stumble into the trees. But Lim seemed to tire of this after an hour, and he gave the rope to the last man in the column.

The soldier who now held the rope was from one of the hill tribes, a large man with a pair of camouflage pants and heavy Army boots he had confiscated. He carried a pair of binoculars slung from his neck, and wore no shirt. In his arm he cradled an M-79 grenade launcher, holding onto the rope with his free hand. He was wearing an Australian bush hat, one side pinned up flat with bone. On the left arm, he wore two thin silver bands, and on the right a U.S. Navy wristwatch. As he pulled on the rope, Reider watched the rope-like muscles ripple across his arms.

In another hour they were climbing the side of a low mountain. The underbrush whipped Reider's face and arms. Already his shoulders ached from the pole and his hands were numb from the wrist cords. Reider flexed his fingers to increase circulation back into his arms. Every fifteen minutes or so, the man holding his rope would look around. His round face would split into a crooked slash, the rope would jerk, and Reider would stumble. By midday, his face and arms were bleeding from the underbrush, and his mouth was sticky and dry. With his tongue, he probed the places where some of his teeth used to be and touched a nerve in one that had not been knocked all the way out.

It occurred to Reider that below, and two minutes away by helicopter, the bodies of the Montagnards would by now be steaming in the sun, and the pigs would be joined by the flies and vultures waiting their turn at the meat.

The shock of having been captured and the loss of his troops began to work on Reider's mind. Somewhere in the back it started—the hate returned. Twice now, Lim had caused him to lose men and friends. He welcomed the hate, letting it grow. A blackness there, buried somewhere in his mind but waiting like a trapped animal. And Reider knew it was there and wanted it to be. He wanted to hold onto it and make it blot out everything that took his attention away from Lim.

Some day, Lim. Some day it will be your turn. Like you said, every dog has his day. . . .

CHAPTER EIGHT

From above, the jungle looked serene. As the helicopters swung in ever-widening circles around the last reporter position of Reider's patrol, the chopper pilots studied the peaceful terrain for any sign of the enemy, alert for the first bright flashes from the trees that would signal flak speeding toward them from guns hidden below.

"Cobra Leader, Cobra Leader, this is Cobra Two. We've spotted bodies in the clearing below. I'm gonna drop down for a looksee."

"Roger that, Jerry. Go ahead. We'll cover you."

Cobra Two banked and swooped in swift descent to treetop level, blowing leaves from the trees and frightening the pigs into the safety of the surrounding jungle wall. The downdraft of its rotors whipped up clouds of red dust, causing the uniforms of the slain to flap and twist around the motionless forms.

"Hank, this is Cobra Two. It looks like Reider's patrol."

"Okay, Jerry," the radio spat back. "I'll go down and make a couple of passes. You boys sit down and take a better look around."

"Roger, Cobra Leader."

"Here I go, Hank. Making my pass at this time. You keep an eye on me and the trees."

The HU-1 moved in with its nose down and both the modified M-60 machineguns on the sides sprayed their 1,200 rounds per minute into the trees. Every fifth round was a tracer steaking red, but the sustained fire succeeded in killing but one pig that had not yet eaten his full. Cobra Two dropped down further and landed in a cloud of dust, the rotor blades just ticking over, but ready to lift off in an instant.

The copilot leaped from the chopper and crouched, holding his tommy gun in front of him. He ran from one body to the next, swinging the gun at the flies and looking furtively into the jungle. He stopped at Kosun's body and turned his face to one side. He ran back to the chopper, giving a thumbs-up signal to the pilot. The copilot scrambled in, leaned out the door and vomited, then pulled himself back in.

"Cobra Leader, Cobra Leader, this is Cobra Two. They're all dead down here. No sign of Reider. Better call Pleiku and tell them to come pick up their people. Let's see if we can find out which way the slopes went."

"Cobra Leader to Cobra Two. Roger. Let's orbit a while and see if we can pick up a trail."

The two helicopters, flying close above the trees, moved away from the clearing and drifted in the direction that Lim's patrol had taken.

"Cobra Two to Leader. Which way you think they went?"

"I don't know, Jerry. Toward the Cambodian border, probably. Maybe down the Ayun River Valley."

The helicopters crossed and crisscrossed the valleys and the low hills, drifting close to the jungle and then away, for perhaps fifteen miles from the clearing where the bodies of Kosun and the Montagnards lay steaming in the heat. Then the helicopters turned west and flew over the muddy water of the Ayun River.

"Two to Cobra Leader. Two to Cobra Leader. I think I've spotted some movement down there along the banks of the river."

"Roger, Two! I see them, too. Let's get 'em!"

The chopper gunboats turned and cut loose, diving and swinging at the trees, sending a barrage of rockets streaming into the jungle to explode and shower hidden men with splinters. They then

sprayed with machineguns over and over again as
they circled above the muddy waters of the river,
diving in toward the jungle. The small figures of
the Viet Cong below the choppers waved their
hands and dived for the sand, shooting ineffec-
tually at the helicopters with rifles and submachineguns.

"Two to Cobra Leader. Is there a Mike Force in
the area?"

"Roger that. They're on the way to join us. Just
keep shredding jungle."

Within minutes, ten helicopters roared into the
area to reinforce the two gunboats, blowing great
swaths in the jungle treetops. Covering themselves
carefully, first one and then another of the choppers set down and discharged the mixed complement of specially trained Montagnards and Green
Berets.

Williams and Sizemore were the first two off
their birds, hitting the ground before the choppers
had touched down. They'd been on a training exercise when their pilot got word that Reider's patrol
had been ambushed.

Their men poured from the Mike Force choppers and sped into the jungle, speeding from tree
to tree as they worked their way toward the area
softened by the raking gunboat fire.

Stunned by the suddenness of the fierce assault,
the VC ran in all directions, completely demor-
alized as they turned to fire sporadically at the
pursuing Mike Force.

The battle raged in bursts. After three murderous exchanges of automatic weapons fire, only four of the Viet Cong were alive. These were taken prisoner by the Green Beret teams, over the protests of the Montagnards, who were eager to see the captives killed. The four were dragged before the Mike Force captain, hands tied behind their backs as they were thrown at the feet of Williams and Sizemore.

Williams had to work hard to control himself, as did Sizemore. They would have liked nothing better than putting a bullet into each of their prisoners' necks. The expression on their faces convinced the prisoners that they were about to die. They trembled uncontrollably on their knees.

Williams turned to Maa Krao, his Montagnard first sergeant, and told him to inform the prisoners they would not be executed if they cooperated. Krao moved over to a prisoner who stared wildly from beneath the blood-soaked bandages encircling his head. The bandage was protecting the bleeding stump of an ear torn away by gunfire during the ambush of Reider's patrol. Seizing the man by his hair, Krao jerked his head backwards, smiling at him through filed-down teeth, commanding him to talk or give up his life. The prisoner moaned in frightened comprehension, shrinking away from the Montagnard who spat in his face, but he said nothing.

Krao turned to Williams: "He is too afraid. He fears I will kill him anyway, talk or no talk."

Sizemore moved over to the VC and placed a cigarette in his mouth. Holding the smoke between shaking lips, the VC attempted a feeble smile, surprised at this unexpected gesture. Perhaps he wasn't going to die. . . .

Williams told Krao to untie the prisoner and one more, offer them water and food, and move the other two captives down to the river bank and tie them to trees.

The Mike Force commander and the Montagnard NCO removed two cans of C rations from their field packs, opened them, and offered the edibles to the startled pair of prisoners. The Montagnard motioned for them to eat. The two prisoners smiled, nodded, and began to eat wolfishly, unmindful of their captors as they concentrated on devouring the C rations.

When the prisoners had finished eating, Sizemore lit two more cigarettes and offered them to the captives. But when he did so, the prisoners cast an apprehensive glance in the direction of their comrades on the river bank. In the glaring eyes of their comrades, they saw hatred—clearly they were traitors for having eaten the Americans' food.

"Caught red-handed," said Sizemore. "Their buddies saw 'em take a bribe."

Williams obtained other cans of C rations, cut them open, and passed them to the two prisoners. But now the food was refused; just as the cigarettes had been.

"I think we have 'em hogtied," grunted Sizemore. "Let's make sure they're branded."

Williams and Sizemore stepped over to the VC

they had fed, shook hands with them, smiled, pounded them on the back and congratulated them in loud Vietnamese for their willingness to cooperate. The VC prisoners stared toward the trees and shook their heads in vehement denial; the captain and the sergeant continued to congratulate them and smile.

The Montagnard NCO then told the two prisoners that they would be taken back to the base and would be confined with their comrades in the same compound. Fear registered in the faces of the two captives who knelt before the Montagnard; the C rations had served not only to sate their appetites but to brand them as traitors to their comrades. There was no escaping the fate awaiting them in that compound; they would be killed. The only avenue of escape was to throw themselves at the feet of the Americans for protection from their own people.

Krao watched his prisoners coolly. He knew their fear of reprisal was paramount now. The Montagnard NCO struggled to control his desire to smile. He told his prisoners of the hut where they would be confined with their comrades, and said that he hoped for their sake that they died quickly at the hands of their vengeful fellow soldiers. Coldly, he watched them try to think matters through while fighting off their rising fears. First one, then the second prisoner began to stammer and then shout to their comrades that they were not traitors, that they had not told the Americans anything of Major Lim or the Green

Beret sergeant Lim held prisoner.

Curses and threats were hurled at the two from the VC tied to the trees. It was evident that the tied VC firmly believed the two who had eaten "GI chow" had talked. And now the two had blurted the name of Major Lim aloud; the fact that the name had been divulged further narrowed their own chances of survival. "Tell them now of how the one called Kosun was slain, for you will envy the animal his death!" shouted one as he strained at the bonds that held him fast. "Traitor!" he screamed. "You and all of your blood will pay for your betrayal!"

The two captives standing before Krao then began to babble incoherently, repudiating their allegiance to the NLF, vowing they were not Viet Cong, swearing they had been forced to don the scanty uniforms they wore and ordered to carry weapons. They swore that they had never killed or hurt anyone.

The Montagnard sergeant interrupted the prisoners' chatter. "Where is Sergeant Reider?" Without hesitation the VC replied they had no idea.

Jeers and insults burst from the prisoners tied to the trees as they saw the rapidly moving lips of the kneeling captives, but Sizemore silenced the disturbance by tossing a hand grenade up in the air and catching it while looking at them fixedly.

The two prisoners began to plead for their lives, and told all they knew of the Major Lim who was commander of a battalion near the border of Cambodia. They did not know where the American sergeant had been taken exactly—they thought perhaps a field hospital because Major Lim would need to have his wounded cared for. Or perhaps the American sergeant had been taken to one of the many underground compounds. It was obvious they had no idea.

The Montagnard sergeant suggested they all go up in a helicopter for a ride at one thousand feet to see how far the two prisoners would bounce. Even that threat did not elicit a more informative response.

Krao had to report to Williams that neither knew for sure where Reider had been taken, or even whether he was still alive. It looked as though Reider would be listed among the lost.

When the interrogation ended, it was apparent to Williams that either the VC would not talk about Major Lim's whereabouts or they simply did not know. It had seemed, in the course of the interview, from their actions and eye movements, the trembling of their lips, and the stark fear in their faces, these VC were more terrified of Major Lim than of the American Special Forces.

Sizemore scratched his grizzled head as he and Williams moved away from the group to talk. He spat and said, "Ain't this the fuckin' shits? It's Lim again! What are we going to do now?"

"I'm fighting the temptation to let the Yards do

as they say and take the prisoners up for some sky-diving lessons, the hard way." Williams squatted down and dug at the ground with his rifle butt. "We are going to find Lim—and Reider if he's alive. I don't care if I have to extend my tour three times. We are going to get that cocksucker Lim if it takes till the war is over. Somehow, someday we'll catch up to them. That's what we're going to do!

"Now get those bastards loaded on the choppers and let's get to work. When the pilot makes his report, I want you to tell him to relay word for Mac to meet us at the chopper pad when we touch down. We're going to burn some ass!"

The Mike Force untied the prisoners and marched them to the waiting helicopters. They were soon airborne, en route to the Special Forces Operational Base.

"Cobra Leader to Momma Bear, Cobra Boat Leader to Momma Bear. We're bringing in some VC. We found Reider's patrol. We didn't find Reider."

Back at the base, where many such reports had been received many times before, several entries were made on charts, comments were added to reports, a telegram was dispatched, friends were informed, drinks were taken, and conversation revolved around someone they had never known well.

For everyone but Williams, Sizemore and Mac, for the rest of the world, that was the end of Sergeant Mike Reider. His usable gear was sent back to the supply room. It would be reissued the next day to some replacements just coming in from Fort Bragg.

Another chapter was closed in the records of the Special Forces. . . .

CHAPTER NINE

Plodding with the rope and the heat through the jungle, Reider alternated between hope and complete despair. Sometimes he knew the choppers would come, and sometimes he doubted anyone had heard a radio report. Perhaps the gunboats would go out. Maybe they would find the clearing and Kosun and his patrol, and maybe they never would. He knew they would follow him if they could; he knew they would search; he knew what they would think if they found the patrol. They would assume he had been captured.

The patrol . . . . Reider hoped that the bodies of Kosun and the rest would not be half-eaten before they were found, and that the pigs and the birds, the ants and the flies, had not been there. But he knew the creatures who fed on carrion were no doubt already tearing the flesh of his men, claiming the cadavers for their own. The thought made his nauseous.

A rifle barrel nudged him in the back. He turned to see the angry face of a VC youth.

Reider's memory cast itself back, separating him from the reality of the moment, drifting toward Fort Bragg, North Carolina, and the Special Warfare Center at Smoke Bomb Hill. The training he had undergone there came back to him, infinitely vivid. He mumbled to himself, "What was it those instructors had to say about the mission of Special Forces . . . had something to do with the Cold War situation, something about planning unconventional warfare in areas not under friendly control . . ." He laughed, but stopped as his neck rubbed against the restrictive hemp of the rope. "Organize, equip, and train . . . direct these forces in the conduct of guerilla warfare . . . advise . . . assist . . . counter guerilla operations in the support of . . . in the support of . . . what was it now, the . . . Cold War objectives. That was it! Hah! But that was then." The laughter erupted again. "And this is now." He chuckled softly. "When was it I first met that bandy-legged little runt Kosun? First time I was assigned to an

A Team, twelve of us stuck in the bushes, forced to make the same mistake the French did—holding an isolated outpost and leaving the rest of the country to the Viets. I must be delirious. Why am I rambling on, so?"

The sun beat fiercely through the trees as Reider stumbled ahead, the smell of his sweat strong in his nostrils as he struggled to breathe deeply and keep control of himself. Through the trees to his right, he thought he could see bamboo-and-thatch houses, but the vegetation obscured his vision. A haze seemed to rise from the foliage itself as Lim's unit plunged ahead. The incessant chatter of birds overhead caught Reider's attention momentarily, but he quickly lost interest in trying to identify the various species and began to thumb through his thoughts again.

It seemed only yesterday—or perhaps last century—that he'd met that tough, stubborn mountain goat, whose name, Ksor Myuen Tonn, was too much of a mouthful and came out Kosun. Oh yeah, in his first patrol assigned to his first A Team—twelve men stuck in the bushes, forced to set up outposts (had he thought this before? It sounded vaguely familiar), left in the middle of the boondocks with no support . . . twelve men, two officers and ten noncoms, an operations sergeant, intelligence, light weapons, heavy weapons, two medics, two radio men and two demo men, everything in pairs so if one got zapped the other could fill in . . . It also made the team able to split into separate units, when necessary.

"Kosun, where were we?" Reider whispered softly. The memory came back to him. . . .

They were on patrol near the Laotian border. He was with one company of Yards and a Viet Chung Ui, a lieutenant in the Luc Long Dac Biet, the Vietnamese Special Forces . . . He was the Viet officers' advisor on the patrol. Yessir, he was ready after all that training he had undergone, he was going to show the Montagnards how to conduct guerilla operations, show those tough little mountain tribesmen who had been fighting in the jungle since Christ was a corporal.

Their first night out from camp, they bivouacked on the crest of the mountain, set their perimeter guards, and went to sleep. Reider could still remember the ache in his legs as those dark Indian looking little Yards had marched the ass off him up and down those damned hills and the cliffs by the river bank, looking for any sign that the VC had crossed . . . He remembered that he had gone to sleep pissed off at the Viet officer. The silly bastard was supposed to be leading the troops, so he was determined that as a patrol leader he would do all the compass and map work. He was okay until they left the river, and then the dumb shit got them lost. They spent three hours climbing that damned mountain, got on top and found out it was the wrong mountain, so Reider asked in his best military-advisor voice for the Chung Ui to show him how to read his map and compass. The Viet did everything perfectly, with one exception: he set the magnetic compass on the steel barrel of his weapon to hold it steady when he took his sightings. They were lucky they were still in Vietnam. They stuck it out on that mountain till morning when, hopefully, they would be able to take new sightings and find out where the hell they were.

Reider's body was still plodding forward, but his spirit was now back on that mountain. He bunked down in a cluster of boulders just off the crest of the ridge, making himself as comfortable as possible. He had just dozed off when he heard a voice whispering, "Trung Si, Trung Si!"

Reider woke up and locked eyes with a smiling, shadowed face with two black coals for eyes. Kosun.

"Trung Si," the voice said. "Le Viet Minh, ils avancent."

"Oh, yeah?" whispered Reider, "where are they coming from?"

Kosun pointed directly down the hill. Reider rubbed his eyes with his hands, wiping the sleep away. He looked down the mountainside searching the trees and bushes and shadows cast by the new moon. A shadow moved. He waited, and it moved again, coming closer up the slope. Reider pointed at the moving shadow. Kosun nodded his head in agreement. Reider pointed to the shadow again and then to himself, as if to say he wanted this one, it would be his first kill. Kosun nodded his head in agreement. The silent shadow slowly worked its way up the mountain. Reider waited. The shape was becoming clearer; now Reider could see the pack on his back, the conical hat of the VC. It seemed as if hours had passed since Reider had first spotted the shadowy firgure. He waited until the figure was about ten meters in front of him and stood up, raised his M-3 sub-machinegun and cut loose with a full burst, then ducked back behind the boulders expecting a wave of return fire. The figure went down with a thump. Nothing else happened.

All the rest of that night, everybody was awake and watching, everyone, that is, but Kosun. Reider admired the little native's nerves, to be able to sleep when a whole jungle full of VC might attack at any minute.

When first light came breaking with a red glow from the east, Reider crawled over the boulders and out into the brush below to get a look at his VC; Kosun watched. Reider reached the position where he figured the Viet had gone down and found . . . a small tree. All the Yards got a laugh out of Reider's kill and told him it was not his fault; if the tree had stayed at the bottom of the hill instead of sneaking up to attack him, it would still be alive. And besides, they all agreed, they had never seen such a dangerous-looking tree before. The specially trained guerilla warfare sergeant from America should not let his conscience bother him. . . .

To this day Reider didn't know whether Kosun had put one over on him. Kosun had never admit-ted anything or shown any reaction when ques-tioned about it . . . and now Kosun lay dead. Reider wondered whether his body had been recovered and sent back to his village so his spirit could rest with those of his fathers. . . .

And he was here, with Lim.

But Reider had learned a great many lessons from Kosun, and between them they had sent a lot of VC to join their ancestors. They had worked well together, he and Kosun, especially after they were able to get away from that advisor bullshit and start running things like equals. Reider had grown to have a deep liking for these people, the Montagnards, and they had liked him and the other Special Forces, too, the bignoses who came and lived with them, ate their food and respected their customs and women. The Americans did not treat them with contempt as did the Vietnamese, and they believed the Americans would not abandon them when the going got rough. One time Hanoi sent a political agitator south to recruit Montagnards, promising that after the Americans and their Vietnamese lackeys had been defeated, they—the North Vietnamese—would set up an independent Montagnard Republic that the Montagnards would rule themselves wtih no interference from the Viets.

A lot of the Yards were buying this agitator's bill of goods. The Special Forces headquarters in Nha Trang wanted a stop put to him. Through ways of their own, they arranged with the Company to send a few patrols across into Laos and Cambodia, using the facilities of Air America. That was the first time Reider'd met big Jay. He'd been their pilot when they'd flown into Long Tien for their briefing and to pick up guides who knew the terrain they'd be working in.

Intell had men in the backcountry villages who'd reported that the Viet agent, one Nguyen Van Thieu, was coming through the next week to speak to influential Montagnard leaders in the village of Plie Djarang across the border in Cambodia, just south of Laos. The brains at Planning and Operations Center decided this was the time to try to intercept him. Several teams would be sent out to lie doggo on the most likely approaches Van Thieu would take to reach Plie Djarang. Reider's unit was one of these teams.

The Spooks wanted Thieu hit or captured before he reached his destination; the last thing they wanted was to start a firefight in Cambodia, particularly in a Montagnard village. Killing any Yard chieftains could start a revolt among the Montagnards that would run the length of Vietnam. Thieu would have to be hit on the way in, and he was sure to be escorted by a strong NVA contingent, probably of at least company strength. The elimination teams were to let all but the unit escorting Thieu pass down the Ho Chi Minh trail; the Montagnard informant said Thieu would be recognized by his height and age: Thieu stood almost five feet ten and had completely grey hair.

Reider and his unit were flown by chopper to a drop zone prepared and secured by an A Team operating in the area. Reider took advantage of their operations to disappear into the jungle cover and head west to his assigned area. It was three days' march through the elephant grass and bush, traveling at night, Indian file, with flankers out to make the best time, his unit broken down into four reinforced squads of fifteen men each.

By the end of the third night, the troops were tired but not exhausted. The first squad moved by, weary but confident of their capabilities in the jungle and ready for the fight they hoped lay ahead. Ambush was their specialty, and few in the world could equal them for patience and ferocity.

Reider moved up to the lead position and crested the mountain with Kosun close on his heels. He looked down into a valley where the elephant grass grew tall and yellow in the early morning sun. It was their assigned area. The trail down into the valley was lined with bamboo clusters too thick for any ambushers to lie in wait, so Reider signaled his men to move forward at a crouch, one squad at a time, down into the valley where they hoped the Viets would come through. They felt the heat build with every step, heat that burned and dried their lungs, as the sun rose higher each minute.

CHAPTER TEN

Reider, still lost in the past, felt the tension once again. This valley was where they would wait. Wait for up to five days, unable to cook or to move except in a crawl. Here, if they were lucky, they would kill or capture an old man and his escort. An old man who could have a hundred thousand Montagnards start a bloodbath throughout the central highlands, perhaps bringing down the Saigon government.

His men crept into the treeline at the base of the

mountain they had just come down, looking like strange, hunchbacked insects in their tiger-striped jungle fatigues and backpacks. Reider had them move by squad into position away from the trail, down the center of the valley. He wouldn't take any chances on NVA flankers blowing his position prematurely. He spoke briefly to Kosun and sent him to find water. Water. Everyone thinks the jungle's got water all over it. Well, maybe some do, but not in Indochina. Each man would need at least three quarts a day, maybe four, depending on the heat. Water and salt tablets would make the difference between heat stroke and health.

They waited. Reider set sentries in trees two miles north of his position with the HT-One Walkie Talkies. They were to report in as soon as they saw any movement, then get out of the trees and head back. Reider figured the Viets would travel by day, considering the age of their big shot, but he needed observation in case they didn't. He had brought a Starlight scope with him. It would allow him to see into the night, although the lenses showed everything in a strange silhouette of green shadows.

Reider had his men dig two-man foxholes and camouflage them. Each hole had a latrine hole dug into the bottom, at least two feet deep . . . A layer of dirt would be shoveled in after each use, keeping the odor down as well as keeping the flies off . . .

They waited . . . silent minds going into a daze,

their eyes red and grainy with strain as they
watched the trail, each day putting another layer
of dust on them. Where the hell did dust come
from in the jungle? No answer presented itself,
but the dust was there, caking lips that had already begun to crack from the heat, no matter how
much water was consumed.

The days ran together. Twice NVA or VC units
came down the trail, but neither had their man, so
Reider let them pass, never knowing how close to
death they were.

After four days, it seemed like a month. Kosun
dozed in the foxhole by Reider, seemingly undis-
turbed by the long hours of boredom. Then Reider
heard a click on the PRC-10 radio, then another,
clicks that said the watchers in the trees had seen
another group coming down the trail from Laos.
Reider raised his hand into the air and snapped
his fingers twice. Instantly, the Yards prepared
themselves, checking their weapons and ammo.
They knew they were not to fight here; the American wanted to wait and follow the Viets until they
bedded down for the night, then hit them while
they were sleeping. So they drew closer to themselves and waited. And Reider watched as his
scouts came in, crawled over to his foxhole and
whispered softly to Kosun.

Kosun turned his face to Reider. "They come,
Trung Si. They come with the old one you said to
watch for."

Reider got out his Zeiss binoculars, adjusted the
centerpiece and focused on the trail, feeling the

sweat run in cool rivulets down his spine, the heat beating down like a hammer, keeping time with the pulse throbbing in his temples.

They came, single file, moving easily down the trail, alert. These were pros. Reider scanned out and away from the main body, searching. Yes, there they were. The flankers, a full squad, about one hundred and fifty meters out from the main force and even with the point man, keeping their distance, weapons at the ready. Most of them were carrying AK-47's, a nice piece of goods that would give a six-inch shot group at one hundred yards. They passed, and the main body of Viets moved across the clear space. Reider watched. There he was. Trung Van Thieu. Reider focused his glasses on the Viet's face. A nice-looking man, like a teacher or a doctor. Reider gave the glasses to Kosun, pointed to the Viet. Kosun took a long look and nodded. The Viet moved out of sight, entering the trees, and Reider kept his count going. The escorting unit, one after another, continued crossing the clear space. One hundred and twenty-five of them, all of them looking good, full equipment, and the latest in Soviet-issue weapons. A couple of the weapons carried by the men directly in front and behind Thieu looked like the new AKM assault rifle. In addition, the Viets were equipped with SKS's and RPD light machineguns and at least three PKS heavy machineguns. Those boys are armed for bear, Reider thought to himself, and you can bet your ass they know how to use their weapons.

Reider waited until the rear guard had passed well out of sight, then leaned over to Kosun and told him to take one other man with him and tail the Viets until they bedded down. "Make sure where the old man sleeps. Draw a chart of their positions—especially those heavy machineguns." Then Reider told Kosun to leave his man there, observing, and to rejoin Reider and the Strikers. They'd be following along the ridge line, well back and out of sight and hearing. Kosun nodded in agreement, crawled into the brush, and disappeared. He reappeared briefly as he stopped at a camouflaged foxhole and one man joined him. Then together they faded into the jungle.

Reider waited an hour to give those bastards plenty of time to get clear before he moved. Squad by squad the Mike Force moved into the treeline, quietly and quickly, taking no chances. They moved, marching silently through the heat of the day, their bodies aching from being cramped in their foxholes for so long, and they marched silently as the sun began to set. The darkness came quickly, settling over the valleys, bringing a hush. The only sounds were the buzzing of insects and the rasping breaths of the men.

Reider moved up behind the point man. They needed all the light they could get, and every time a cloud cast its shadow through the trees they would wait until the moon once again showed the way. Mosquitoes began their humming drone. Skin itching from the bites, breath rasping from a parched throat, Reider felt the elation only a hunter can know as he nears his quarry. And then he knew he was not alone. Raising his eyes, he saw a shadow move in front of him. His finger automatically tightened on the trigger, till he heard the soft, familiar voice saying, "Trung Si, I am here . . ." Kosun. The little bastard moved like a ghost in the night. Reider passed the word for the squad leaders to come forward while the men rested. One by one, the four squad leaders gathered around Reider and Kosun.

"Trung Si," said Kosun, "the Viets camp two kilometers away. They even now prepare their evening rice; they are confident and talk loudly among themselves, but there is no drinking."

Reider asked for the disposition of the troops. Kosun took out a small piece of paper and scanned it before answering.

"They have set out blocking forces of five men each at each end of the trail, about three hundred meters from each end of the campsite. They have also set perimeter security out, each man and a comrade have a foxhole. Beyond them, outside the perimeter about forty meters, are four listening posts, each with two men. These posts are marked here and here on the paper. The heavy machineguns are set close to the inner camp, one on each end of the trail and one pointing to the mountain on which we sit. Only a few sentries are on the river side, for across the river is Laos, and they know there will be no attack from there. The old man sleeps in the only tent near the river. There are two guards at his position. I saw no more."

Reider nodded his head, glad that Kosun had decided to speak English for a change. "You saw enough, you raggedy-ass little heathen. Good, Kosun. You are one with the jungle, and I am glad you are here to be my eyes and ears. So, my little tiger, let us prepare for the night ahead. Tell the men to sleep in turns, no smoking, no cooking tonight. They shall feed and drink on the blood of their enemies. Now leave me the paper and return to the man you left to watch. And wait for us to join you. Rest while you can, little tiger, I will have need for the long claw that you carry this night."

Reider sat and thought. The Viets were strong and well-positioned, except for the river. Okay, then, he would use the river.

Reider spoke to his squad leaders. "Okay, Heng Sor. You will be on the right flank with your squad. Xuan, you take the center, and Krao, your squad, the left. No mortars until five minutes have passed after the first shot. Got that?" All heads nodded in agreement. "Fourth squad will be the ones with the 60mm mortars. I want you to use white phosphorus to start with, five rounds of each in the camp center. Then switch to high explosive rounds, and spread them out, random firing over the target area. Machinegunners, set for grazing fire. Each of the first three squads take out two men each to get rid of the listening posts. No guns; use your blades. Then gunners take over the listening posts for your firing positions. No heroics.

"After Kosun and I get the old man, we'll pull

back around and rejoin you on the crest. There's a natural incline at the point we make the hit to withdraw. Give me ten minutes of concentrated fire and pull back under cover of the mortars. Set positions on the hillside. You can expect them to attack and pursue as soon as they find the old man's gone. If we can channel them to this gully, we stand a pretty good chance of wasting a lot of them. Radioman, as soon as the first shots are fired, you make contact with the SFOB. Best set up on the top of the mountain and use a jungle antenna. Tell HQ we want evacuation at LZ Jupiter at 0700 hours. Alternate ill be LZ Venus at 1200 hours. Okay, we will hit them at exactly 0300 hours. Take out the listening posts at 0245, then cut loose with MGs at 0300. Kosun and I will move out, circle the camp, and come in from the river."

Reider sent a runner to bring Kosun back in, and he and Kosun moved down the valley, reaching the river bank without incident. They lay with their faces in the cool water, letting their pores soak up all they could, then rested in the mud and reeds by the bank and waited, counting the minutes while the night dragged on. The decaying odor of the mud was rich from the rains and dying vegetation.

Reider checked his Seiko, motioned to Kosun and moved out into the river waist deep, now holding his Thompson submachinegun over his chest. The currents of the river tugged at his pants while the black mud sucked at his boots like a living thing. Kosun followed, keeping to the shadows.

Time dragged like the mud, slow and pulling, but at last the moon was going down behind the crests of mountains; in a few more minutes there would be total blackness. Reider checked his watch again: twenty minutes before the fireworks start. As the moon disappeared, Reider and Kosun moved further out into the river, holding their weapons and ammo over their heads. The dark waters reached up to their chests.

As they neared the Viet positions, Reider could hear soft voices making the sing-song sounds of Vietnamese, and then he spotted a soft glow from the old man's tent. Thanks for the light, old man. We need all the help we can get.

Reider and Kosun moved in closer to the bank, lowering their bodies down as they reached the shallows until they were on the river bank, lying in the cool mud, ears straining for sounds.

Reider checked his watch again. Ten minutes to go. They crawled out of the mud and into the high grass, and Reider's eyes searched the darkness; his guts churned as if a cold hand had reached inside and was squeezing them and then letting them go. They moved closer to the light that glowed from within the tent, until Reider could just pick out the two sentries on guard there. He nudged Kosun, pointed to the one on the left, and made a sliding motion across his throat with his finger. Even in the darkness, Reider could feel Kosun smile.

Together they crawled closer to the tent, eyes never leaving their targets. Reider pulled his combat knife from its leather sheath, set his

Thompson in the grass, and slowly rose to his knees. Kosun withdrew his cutdown version of a butcher knife.

As the two sentries moved close together, they sprang. Reider grabbed his man around the throat and slid the blade of his knife deep into the Viet's back, just below the last rib on the right, and then turned it in to the left and drew it back out, severing the spinal cord and slashing through kidneys.

Reider rose from the dead man, and looked across to Kosun. He had finished off his man and was taking time to remove the ears for a trophy. Two quick slices, and they were off and in Kosun's pockets. Reider motioned for Kosun to get their weapons. As Kosun picked up the submachineguns, Reider moved to the tent and looked through the flap. The old man had heard nothing. He sat at a table writing, making notes for his speech to the Yard chieftains, no doubt. Well, it didn't look as if he would be needing them.

Reider scratched at the tent flap and whispered, "Ong! Ong! Shh! Shh!"

The old man raised his head at the sound and asked in Vietnamese, "What is it?"

Reider, standing in the darkness, whispered, "Shh!"

The old man turned down his light and moved to the flap to see what was happening. Reider grinned in the dark. That's right, big boy, come to papa. The Viet stuck his head outside, Reider came down with a chop to the neck that knocked the old man out instantly. Reider quickly moved inside the tent, picked up the old man's papers, and stuck them inside his fatigue jacket.

By the time he came out, Kosun had the old man gagged and tied. Kosun put the man on his shoulders in a fireman's carry and walked down into the black waters of the river. Reider followed, gun at the ready, covering Kosun and his package. He, too, entered the black swirling waters, and they began to move away from the site.

As they reached midstream, Reider's squads opened up, sending round after round into the camp, tracers piercing the night with their burning light. Reider could hear the Viets screaming in confusion, but already they were returning the fire. Good troops, confused but no panic. He'd better get their asses out of there. The sounds by the tent told him the VC had already found the old man missing.

Reider and Kosun left the river, moved between the Viet rearguard and the main camp, and headed for the mountain, carrying their burden with them. And now came the mortars into the camp, blooming into eye-searing light as the white phosphorous shells burst amid the Viets. Reider's troops were laying down a tremendous amount of fire. As he reached the ravine leading up the mountain, he could hear the heavier, throaty CHUH-CHUH sound of the PKS machineguns beginning to assert themselves.

Reider took Thieu from Kosun and began to climb, grabbing unseen vines and roots to pull himself up the mountain. How high was this

sucker? Chest aching with the strain, he reached
the top, turned and looked back down into the
valley. The mortars had stopped firing. The only
fire being sent into the Viets was that of individual
squads as they leapfrogged back, covering one
another in their withdrawal, steady and controlled. Reider nodded in approval. His boys were
good. They were doing it by the book.

One by one, heads began to appear in the dark
shadows as his men reached the crest of the ridge
where Reider waited for them. First up were the
mortar men. He had them set up immediately and
start lobbing rounds down into the valley. He
needed to slow the VC up. As more men joined
them, he turned his prisoner over to them, with
strict instructions they were not to hurt Thieu
unless it looked as though he would be rescued by
his comrades. As Reider's men reached the ridge,
he called for a count. Good. They were all in, and
only one had a minor gunshot wound in the thigh.
But he would be able to walk.

Reider called for a halt to his return fire, knowing that in the dark the Viets would follow the line
of least resistance to the hilltop. The squads regrouped and set up their weapons to cover the
approach. Reider detailed men to each side in case
Charley tried to flank him. What time was it now?
0415. It would be light in two more hours. He
needed to slow them up. They had reacted faster
than he thought they would. Reider gave instructions for his mortar crews to use their two rounds
each of illuminating shell when he gave the word.

All grew quiet on the ridge as they waited. The only sound was occasional gunfire from below as the Viets fired at shadows. Then he could hear them stumbling and swearing as they clawed their way up the ravine.

Reider waited until he could make out the dim shapes below him and gave the signal to the mortar crews. As the first blinding bursts of light exploded over the valley, Reider's Strikers poured down a hail of deadly fire. Ricochets sang off the rocks. Reider yelled for grenades, and one after another, as fast as their pins could be pulled, the cheering Montagnards tossed them down into the ravine. The grenades exploded with muffled thumps among the tightly packed Viets, blasting faces into mindless rags of bloody jelly, sending shreds of shrapnel into stomach and spines.

"Give it to them!" screamed Reider. "Kill the bastards!" And kill they did. The Viets couldn't face this opposition and pulled back out of range.

"They'll try to flank us next," Reider said, "so pack up and move out. Form a running U, mortar crew to the front." And they ran, gaining time on the enraged Viets below. The time was 0515. The pickup was set for 0700 at LZ Jupiter.

"Run, you raggedy-ass heathens," yelled Reider. "Run! Drop your packs. Only weapons and ammo." Run they did, stumbling into trees and thickets, vines whipping across their faces, leaving deep, burning cuts.

Behind them, Reider could hear gunfire as the NVA troops assaulted the ridge only to find no one

there. Reider herded his men along, keeping them
together. He paused for a moment, picked up a
pack that had been thrown aside, set a grenade
under it, pin pulled, the weight of the pack holding
the handle down. Anyone who lifted the pack
would have his way of life changed. "No panic,
now," he told his men as he trotted to their front.
"We almost have it made. Only a little while to
go." Reider took a compass reading, and led his
men toward the LZ.

Dawn was beginning to break, and the first red
light of day was seeping through the canopy overhead. Reider signaled for his men to slow down.
They could make good time now with the coming
light. Reider looked back. There was no sign of the
pursuing Viets, but he knew they were coming.
Walk three minutes, run two. The Mike Force
pushed their way through the jungle. The Viet
politico had long since regained consciousness,
but was making no trouble as the Yards dragged
him along with them. 0630. Thirty minutes to go.
They neared the LZ and Reider called for the
radio. He tried to raise his recovery choppers:
"Nurse Maid, Nurse Maid. Are you ready to
evacuate? Over."

And then over the air came a crackling response:
"Roger, Orphan, read you three by three. But
we're coming closer. Are you ready to evacuate?
Over."

"Roger, Nurse Maid. We will be at the LZ in ten,
repeat ten minutes. Can you provide any air
cover? Over."

"Roger, Orphan. We figured you would have some unwanted company so we brought a friend. He should be joining us about five minutes from now. Do you copy? Over."

"Roger, Nurse Maid. This is Orphan. Out."

Reider and his men struggled over one last hill and there was the LZ below, the nice clear piece of ground where the choppers would set down for them. The sight gave new strength to the Strikers, and they raced to the LZ, dragging their prisoner with them. When Reider reached the LZ, he could hear the choppers in the distance, coming closer. Quickly, he set up a perimeter to give cover while they boarded the copters. The Strikers threw themselves to the ground in a circle around the landing zone, weapons pointing out to the treeline surrounding them.

The choppers came in, their blades blowing up great clouds of red dust and grass. As the first bird set down, Reider picked up Thieu and threw him into the door by the crew chief's feet. "Take care of this one!" he yelled. "And get his ass back to the SFOB in Pleiku? Now!" Reider slapped three Strikers on the butts as they clambered into the chopper with Thieu, as it lifted off, it blasted Reider with stinging bits of dirt and debris. By now other choppers were settling into the clearing, picking up his men. But then came a whining sound, repeating itself over and over, as small-arms fire began to reach into the choppers. The NVA had reached them. As more of Reider's men got on board the Hueys, he had less on the ground to give supporting fire.

Reider grabbed the radio from his comm man and yelled into the mouthpiece over the roar of the choppers: "Nurse Maid, where's that support you said was coming?"

Crackling back into his ear, a Georgia drawl replied, "Don't sweat it, big boy, you just tell us where you want it, 'cause Puff the Magic Dragon's on his way!"

Reider raised his eyes to the sky and saw a C-47 orbiting overhead. "Hot damn!" he yelled back into the mouthpiece. "Okay, Puff, lay it on the east side of the LZ as close as you can get."

"Roger, big boy. Just like you want it."

Reider signaled his remaining Strikers to pull back, and the Gooney Bird circled around. From its side came a high-pitched hum as Puff let loose with its electronically controlled Gatling guns firing in three-second relays, sending down what looked like a solid sheet of fire into the eastern edge of the LZ.

Reider stared in wonder as trees disintegrated under the impact of the many thousands of rounds a minute being hurled down from the obsolete-looking aircraft overhead, a solid humming barrage of fire that blasted everything in its path to dust or splinters. Reider didn't like to think about what it left of the men that it struck. And as Puff laid down the protective shield over the LZ, Reider and the last of his men boarded the choppers and rose up over the trees, flying low and fast away from the LZ.

They had made it. Reider smiled at the memory. That had been a hairy one.

But the Silver Star he had received for that operation was not going to help him now. The only help he could count on was himself. . . .

CHAPTER ELEVEN

Reider was jerked back to reality by the rope. The Viet pulling him had yanked it hard, almost bringing him to his knees, and Major Lim was moving back toward him.

"Ah, Sergeant," said Lim, "I see you cannot keep up. I must warn you, Sergeant, I am losing my patience. There is really very little reason for keeping you alive. Sometimes we learn from prisoners, but I fear I have already learned more about American tactics than you know."

They were leaving the thick jungle and slipping down a low ridge toward a river. Lim kept up his running monologue, sometimes talking about the time he had spent in the States as an Exchange Officer, sometimes remarking on the way he had been treated, and sometimes snarling to his men.

"There, Sergeant," he said, "are the waters of the Ayun River." The Major pointed down a low hill toward the banks. The river was very dirty this close. Reider had seen it many times from the air. In places not near the Cambodian border, and on maps, it was clearer and flowed very wide and quite slowly. In some places where the Viet Cong did not have crossings, he and other American forces swam and enjoyed themselves. But here at this point, where there was obviously a VC crossing, the river was brown and dirty, and green scum lined the banks. It was also very narrow, and at this time of the year, before the monsoon season, it was low and sluggish. The patrol moved down the hill toward the bank.

"I like talking with you, Sergeant," said Lim. "You see, I do not need to be at the front of my troops. They are well trained, don't you agree?"

Reider did not reply.

"Sergeant, you must learn to pay attention. I would like to have your military opinion. Don't you think them excellent?"

"No," Reider replied at last. "Not by a long shot."

"No?" Lim grimaced. "Who lost a patrol? A few scratches, Sergeant, that's all my men suffered.

Where are your men?"

Reider was about to answer, but then a familiar sound came to him very faintly. At first he thought he was imagining it, because he wanted to hear it so much. And Lim did not hear what Reider heard. Reider tried to keep Lim talking.

"You were lucky, Lim, just lucky."

"Lucky, Sergeant?" The remark brought the Major up short. He scowled. "A strange thing for you to say. But then perhaps not so strange, since you are the loser. 'Sore loser,' is that how you say it in your country? Poor loser. But loser, nevertheless. And yet it seems you still have some small part of luck with you, Sergeant. You are lucky. You are not where your filthy Montagnard is."

"Well," said Reider, but suddenly one of the VC was yelling, and Lim yelled back, "Into the jungle! Quickly! Straighten the grass!" He waved his arms. Two VC jerked Reider down low.

The choppers came in low, hunting and ducking in circles above the river and jungle. They came closer and hovered a few hundred yards away just above the trees, and then swept in, shooting rockets and machinegun fire all across the banks of the Ayun River and into the underbrush and Lim's patrol. Lim grabbed Reider by the hair, tilted his head back and said, "Sergeant, do not get ideas about signaling. If you move one muscle, you won't live to get their attention."

The choppers were directly overhead, the wind from their blades beating on the jungle roof like a hammer.

Reider tensed and pulled his knees tight against his chest. He felt the muscles in his back tighten as he dipped and brought his arms and the pole up into Lim's groin. Lim doubled over, holding his testicles and screaming with agony.

Reider rose to his feet and stumbled past the major into the open space by the river bank. Behind, lying on the ground, screaming, his right hand between his legs, Lim struggled to get his Tokarev service pistol out of its polished black leather holster. Reider was waving as well as he could with the pole between his arms, wagging it as if it were a flag. And then he felt the hot pain, the pain of a slug. It hit his leg, and the day began to go dark. His last thought was the hope that he had ruptured the bastard.

When Reider came to, he was lying in the underbrush. The leaves about him were bloody. Standing over him were a VC and Major Lim with his left arm in a crude sling made from his belt. There was no one around but some bodies. Lim's arm was a twisted, awkward, angular thing, and Lim's uniform jacket was red with blood. He began to curse at Reider in Viet, and then suddenly he switched to English, his face contorted and black eyes staring.

"Sergeant, you are responsible for this, and I will find a way to make you pay for your mistake. You will be very sorry. You have caused my men to be killed, you have caused me to be wounded, and now I have you, Sergeant. I want you right now. I want you to live, and you will live, Sergeant.

But every moment that you do, I am going to make you know you would rather have died with your Montagnards than to be here right now with me. You have cost me my patrol. You lost your patrol, Sergeant. All you lost were some slopes. But for me, these are my people—not someone from across the ocean. And despite what you would like to think, Sergeant, not people from China or Russia or Korea—but my people, Sergeant. One of the men that was killed I grew up with, and I would have had him killed easily and with no loss to my conscience had it been necessary, Sergeant, because this is a war of liberation. But it was not necessary, Sergeant, not this time; and he is dead. Many of my men are dead, and you and I are going to live, because right now we need each other. We will need each other for a long time, I think."

Reider was barely conscious. He was not even quite sure where he was. All he could see from where he lay was Lim, the blood on the leaves, and the chopped-up trees. He thought he heard Montagnard voices, and then all went black and he heard nothing. Then he was awake again, or seemed to be awake, and he thought he heard choppers. But it was from a long distance, and the sound was not very clear, and then everything went black again. He awoke and time became an animal's unconscious marking of intervals waking and sleeping. And then he felt a jerk at his neck, and Lim's face was close to his again, the eyes black and bright.

"Sergeant, don't die. Your friends are about to

leave. It is only fifteen miles to the Cambodian
border, and we will make it—the two of us. And
you will wish I had left you here to die. You will
wish that every minute from now on. You are
going to pray for death. There will be a beauty in
it. From now until the end of your life, there will
be no beauty unless you die, and you will not die
before I am ready."

Reider was still having flashes of darkness, and
the pain in his leg was beginning to make him
nauseous. Lim jerked the rope still around
Reider's neck and somehow Reider managed to
crawl down the jungle path toward the beach. He
began to vomit after a few yards, and Lim turned
back to him. "Not yet, Sergeant. You will crawl, or
I will pull until you begin to strangle, so crawl.
Crawl."

The VC with Reider reached to help with the
leash. Lim struck his hand. "No, he's mine."

Slowly, painfully, Reider moved one knee before
the other, and he and Lim moved slowly out of the
underbrush and onto the beach. The VC stood by
the bank and watched over them, SKS at the
ready. Lim sat by the edge of the water, washing
the blood from his arm, and splashing the dirty
brown water onto his face. Reider moved the remaining ten feet to the river and stuck his head in
the water. The rush of the current and the warmth
made him sleepy. He felt the softness of it on his
face and opened his mouth. Lim jerked the rope.
"No, Sergeant. No water. You will get sick, and I
don't want you sick. We will rest for ten minutes,

that is all. Then we walk. You had better try your
leg. It's a long walk, and there will be times I
cannot help you, but together we will get there."

Lim stuffed small scraps of cloth into the bullet
hole in Reider's left leg.

Reider lay on the warm beach feeling the sun
above and smelling the jungle, and hearing the
sounds the water made as it moved in and out
among the rocks. The pain in his leg was gone—
disappeared into a dull ache that twisted him in-
voluntarily when he moved. His leg had no feeling
below the kneecap. His feet were already starting
to bleed from cuts made earlier in the day. His
arms were heavy, and he wished he could sleep.
Lim hovered near him, not speaking, staring into
his face and breathing heavily. When Lim moved,
he groaned and held his arm.

"Come, Sergeant, it is time," said Lim after a
while, slowly rising to his feet. He pulled Reider
up by the rope; Reider's leg collapsed. Lim
removed the rope and threw it in the water.

"Come on, Sergeant. Lean on me. We will walk
together."

Their silent escort leading, they staggered down
the beach, keeping just inside the water's edge,
their feet leaving wet prints in the sand. Reider
fell twice and Lim pulled him up. Blackness and
light were warring again. He wanted nothing more
than to lie by the water, drinking the flat-tasting
brown liquid and letting the sun warm him until
the blackness came and stayed and he wouldn't
have to take another step. Late in the afternoon,

some time—Reider was not sure—they stopped
again and rested for an entire hour.

And then it was night, and the sounds of the
jungle were loud. They rested by the side of the
river. Around eight o'clock, Reider blacked out
again for what seemed like an hour or two and
came to with Lim shouting at him and splashing
water in his face. "Not now, not now. Sleep later!"

They staggered on, weaving along the bank, occasionally falling into the water. The moon came
up about nine, illuminating the tops of the trees
and reflecting from the surface of the river. Lim
was moving more slowly now, falling, too, and taking a timeless interval to recover.

Some time after midnight Lim fell again and
spoke. His voice was slurred and came in a whisper. "We sleep now, Sergeant. Sleep." He used his
belt to tie Reider to a tree, and lay like a child
curled against the trunk, his hand against his
cheek for a pillow, his twisted left arm cradled by
his right.

For a moment, Reider thought of escape, but his
arms were heavy, and his mind too fogged to
think. He drifted into a mindless sleep in which
pain and flashes of gunfire flickered on the edges
of his mind.

When morning came, Reider couldn't move. His
back was numb from waist to shoulder, and his
hands were a dull red from being tied too tightly.
Lim was not awake. The other VC was gone. The
sounds of the night had gone, the day creatures
were out, and the sun threw shafts of light into the

thick jungle ahead. Reider was thirsty. His mouth was dry, and he seemed to have no spit left. He blacked out again.

"Up, Sergeant," said Lim. "Get up."

Reider nodded his head against the tree and fell asleep again. Lim slapped him across the face and then hit him in the head with his belt. The sharp stinging pain brought Reider awake again. He tried to speak. Nothing came out except a groan that hurt his throat and did not pass his lips. His mouth was swollen, full with dried blood. He gagged and tried to vomit. Lim pulled him by the arm, almost tenderly, like a child trying to get a grown-up to join a game. Together they staggered further into the jungle. All Reider could think of was water—the taste of fresh water and the way it felt going down his throat, and the coolness of it in his stomach. Lim was mumbling about a river crossing, searching the jungle paths for a shortcut across a large looping S in the river.

It was Reider who first found the water hole. He croaked and managed to say, "Water."

Lim dropped him and knelt by the black pool scooping his hand in and out. Lim stretched his hand toward Reider, something black in the palm. "You want some water, Sergeant?" he asked. He was speaking slowly, patiently.

"Yes. Water."

Lim grabbed Reider's hand and dragged him to the edge of the pool. "You will feel much better when you have something to drink."

"Better. Water." Reider gasped.

Lim took him by the hair and shoved his face into the pool. Reider couldn't move. He tried to drink, but the water only made him gag. He felt a sting on his face and several around his mouth. Lim finally pulled him back from the edge, slowly reached his hand up to Reider's face, pulled off a leech from the skin above the right eye, and showed it to Reider. He was too weak to move, but just lay by the side of the pool, Lim grinning at him. He felt the pain in his face and knew many leeches were sucking his blood.

"Jesus, God," said Reider.

"They seem to like you, Sergeant," said Lim. "They have grown on you. Stay awake."

From somewhere in the back of his mind, Reider managed to find an energy he didn't know he had. He frantically scraped his face in the dirt around the pool to dislodge the leeches. He was moving his head from side to side like a dog wiping his nose.

Lim laughed nastily, pitilessly. "Let me help you, Reider." He tore them from Reider's face, one by one.

"The best way," said Lim, "is to burn them off. But we are without matches, Sergeant."

When the last leech had been removed, Reider sat shaking uncontrollably for a few moments and stared at Lim, who sat beside the pool, his face darkly outlined against the jungle. Lim seemed to be listening for something.

Reider groaned and tried to sit up.

Lim pointed his pistol at Reider and motioned for him to be silent, moved closer and shoved

Reider's head into the dirt. "Not a sound, Ser-geant. Not a sound. There is someone moving toward us. Silence."

In a moment Lim released Reider's head and began pulling him away from the water hole, but Lim was weak and Reider had no strength left in him. Their progress was measured in inches. The sounds of men hacking their way through the bushes beyond the pool were loud now, but the voices were faint and high-pitched. Lim got his good arm around Reider's neck and tugged him behind a tree. Reider nearly blacked out, but fought to remain conscious as Lim aimed his revolver toward the sounds. For a few moments Reider strained to identify the language drifting toward them, but grew tired of trying. He raised his arms and slashed at Lim's pistol as powerfully as he could. Lim fell, and Reider crawled to the edge of the path and cried weakly, "Here! Here!"

The undergrowth parted and Reider lay with his head a few inches from a boot. It was the most beautiful boot he had ever seen. It had a thick sole and was stitched, and it resembled the kind of footwear he had been issued during basic training, the kind he had worn himself as a trainee. No sight ever looked so good to him. He cried, waiting for the shot he knew would come, the shot that would take Lim's last breath. Reider wished he were strong enough to shoot Lim himself—to have the satisfaction of using Lim's own pistol to leave a slug in the middle of his brain. Reider sobbed in relief. . . .

CHAPTER TWELVE

The gunfire didn't come. He raised his eyes from the ground, along the laces of the boot, to see black pajamas and a thin Mongolian face and a Chinese-made submachinegun.

One of the soldiers kicked him.

"We are home, Sergeant," said Lim. "We have come home. Bac-si."

"No bac-si," the tallest of the Chinese, the one whose boots Reider had thought American, said.

"Bac-si . . . bac si . . ."

Lim collapsed.

Reider's senses suddenly sharpened.

One moment Lim had been the taunting, sadistic master. The next his "Bac-si, bac-si, bac-si" was the sound of a phonograph running down, and he would have fallen into the dirt had not two of the Chinese soldiers caught him. His eyes were closed. He was unconscious. The crude sling under his twisted arm began to pulse red with arterial blood.

The gutsy son of a bitch. He had held out to the very last minute. Admiration welled up in Reider.

"No bac-si," the Chinese repeated stupidly.

The son of a bitch was going to die. Reider could feel the certainty in his own brain. Lim's face was draining of color. He had the look of death about him. At that moment the blood spurting from the shattered arm fell on the hand of one of the Chinese holding him. The soldier looked dazed.

At that moment, Lim recovered consciousness. His eyes were beginning to fog as they focused on Reider, but his voice had a surprising clarity for a dying man.

"We have no doctor here, Sergeant, so it appears that I am going to die." There was no expression on his face as his fogging eyes held Reider, then turned to the Chinese lieutenant. He gave the lieutenant his orders in a slow, distinct voice. The effort seemed to revive him. When he turned back to Reider there was black malice in his glazing eyes as he translated his order into English. "The second I die, the lieutenant will kill you Reider and bury you at my feet—as ancient man did with his dogs and slaves so that they might serve him in the next life." Lim grinned slowly and wickedly at Reider. "You see, Sergeant, where I go, you go." He began to laugh weakly, but before he could finish the laugh he was unconscious. He was dying.

Reider stood for a moment in silence. The bastard meant it.

The Chinese patrol, which numbered less than a dozen men, took Lim and Reider into the tiny Cong village just beyond the water hole. There were maybe a dozen villagers. One in particular, a short old man who looked as ancient as the jungle itself, seemed to be the head man. Reider looked at him. "What's your name?"

"Tah."

"You number one man?"

"Yes."

Reider tried to sort out the ratings and rank of the Chinese. The tall Chinese—the one with the boots Reider had first seen—was a lieutenant and apparently in charge. He probably didn't speak English, but hell—it was worth a try.

"Your major's dying. Aren't you going to do anything about it?"

"No bac-si, Sergeant. There is nothing we can do." So he did speak English!

"Like hell there isn't. That arm must come off or he'll die."

"Are you a medic, Sergeant?"

"No, but I have had some training. I helped out

once on an amputation. I've got a pretty good idea
of what's involved.''

Again the eyes of the Chinese lieutenant searched deeply into Reider. He turned to his men and
gave several short orders. Then he looked at
Reider. "I have told them to help you, to give you
whatever you need.''

He seemed to wait for Reider's reaction. When
there was none, his voice took on an odd quality,
half-distaste, half-compassion. "After all, Sergeant, if Major Lim dies, you die. So I suggest that
you prepare yourself. It is probably best this way.
If I—or one of my men—operated, we might be
held responsible for the major's death. But if you
do it and he dies, no blame can be put on us. And
besides, there seems to be a strange association
between you and our major. I think that if he were
conscious he would prefer it this way himself.
What do you need?''

Reider thought.

"Bring everything you've got. Especially any
American supplies or médicines.'' He searched his
mind. Lim had had an American survival kit. "Get
that survival kit.''

The lieutenant cut his bonds, and the pole
dropped to the ground. Reider rubbed his arms;
the relief was agony, or the agony was relief; he
wasn't sure which.

Ten minutes later, they had Lim stretched out
on a makeshift table in one of the huts and Reider
was preparing to amputate the arm. A young
Chinese soldier stood by to assist; three more

stood ready to hold Lim still.

Reider cast his mind back to the camp at Plei Jrong, where he'd assisted Mac Rigsby in amputating a Montagnard's foot just above the ankle. Mac did what he called a guillotine amputation—the quickest kind. Nothing fancy, just getting it off as soon as possible. That would be the way to go.

He examined the instruments and medicines available to him and prepared to make his first cut. Selecting a long thin knife with a slightly curved blade, he soaked the blade in alcohol and swabbed down the area he was going to cut. He gave Lim a quarter grain of morphine intravenously, took another look, gave a long sigh, and. . . . Damn! The first cut would be the hardest. Stay with me, Mac, he thought. I may need some help.

Reider made his first cut two inches below the tourniquet, about four inches below the elbow, slicing through the tissue. Quickly readjusting the tourniquet, he irrigated the wound with raw alcohol. There was no sterile water, and that suited Reider just fine. He might have to save the bastard's life, but there was no reason for him to make it easy on him. He felt better. Whistling between his lips, he sliced more deeply, cutting until he came to a large artery. Okay. He tied it off with a piece of thread. Mac had been right. Most of the veins just popped back inside the meat when they were cut, the surrounding muscle tissue clamping down on them, keeping them from excessive bleeding. About all that remained was a little seepage. Reider tied off several large bleeders. Then one more cut, and the bones were exposed.

Now for the saw.

Stay with me, Mac.

First irrigating the wound with the alcohol, Reider examined it briefly. He reached into the survival kit and withdrew the saw, a thin, narrow, flexible saw, provided for jungle survival, with a wooden handle at either end of the blade. It could cut through a small twig or thick bamboo or heavy vine—or cut through the two major bones of a forearm. He injected morphine into the major, another quarter grain.

Reider clasped the saw with both hands. In a fast, whipping motion, the saw bit hard into the bone. Lim jerked, but the edge held firm. Reider did not stop until the smaller of the two bones was severed. Lim went into massive spasms. Reider irrigated. With gauze he removed the crusty bone dust from the teeth of the saw. He dipped the blade into alcohol and attacked the larger bone. The young Chinese soldier wiped Reider's brow. In two minutes the arm dropped off, leaving a ragged end protruding from Lim's flesh. The soldier snatched the arm as it rolled off the table.

Reider took a deep breath. "Get rid of it," he ordered.

He sawed at the ragged bone to smooth it. The marrow was explosed. Reider retched. He had to pack it fast, but he had nothing. If it got infected, Lim was dead for sure. He looked up, questioning.

A deadly pause.

The soldier stuttered in Vietnamese. Reider did

not understand. "What?" he asked.

He stuttered again.

"Can you say it in English?" Reider asked desperately. "English? Damn it, get that lieutenant."

Reider looked down at Lim who was still jerking mildly. The men who held Lim did so with eyes tightly closed. All were pale. Reider held the arm stump up, keeping it just above the level of the tourniquet.

The lieutenant appeared.

"Tell him."

The young Chinese stuttered to the lieutenant.

"What did he say, damn it?"

"Candle," the lieutenant answered.

Reider almost dropped the arm as he reached across Lim to slap the young Chinese off his feet.

"Damn! Damn! Damn!" he shouted. "Get the fucking candle!"

Silence.

"A candle!"

They were not comprehending.

"Get a fucking candle!" Reider screamed at the top of his lungs. "Candle!"

The lieutenant ran.

In seconds the whole village echoed with the screams of "candle!" A young boy appeared from nowhere. He stopped a safe distance from the table. Reider stared at the boy. Tah's son? He looked like the old man. Reider thought he remembered seeing such a boy earlier in the day—a hundred years ago. . . . The boy took two steps forward and withdrew from his pocket a small grey stick. Reider reached for it as the lieutenant and Tah came racing back on the scene.

"There is no—" the lieutenant began, but stopped himself as the boy timidly handed Reider what appeared to be a piece of wax candle. Reider snatched it. The boy stood frozen. Reider looked back up, asked for a match, and was surprised at the boy's obvious fear.

"You have just saved a man's life. Your major's life," he comforted. "You were a good boy."

The boy opened his mouth to speak and chose instead to run away.

Reider got a match from the lieutenant, melted wax, and packed it into the bones. Twelve minutes had elapsed. He released the pressure tourniquet. He had missed no bleeders. It was a good operational stump. He pulled down the loose skin which he had carefully left, and covered the entire exposed stump with the healthy tissue. He inserted a cotton gauze drain and held the skin tightly in place. He asked for a boot lace, adding, "One of Lim's." He tied the covering skin with the boot lace. The gauze stayed in place. The wound did not bleed.

The operation was over.

"Let him go," Reider said.

For the first time in fifteen minutes, the three men who had held Lim by each leg and his head opened their eyes, blinking.

The bodyguard spoke first. "Bac-si! Number one. Number one bac-si!"

Reider smiled, pleased with himself. The young

soldier bowed deeply—with much respect. "Now I thank my gods."

Reider nodded. He'd thank Mac.

The small group gathered about Reider, turning him away from Lim. He leaned back against the table, supporting his weight on his hands, and let his head fall back. He was exhausted and exhilarated at the same time.

The Chinese lieutenant walked up to Reider and said, "You are truly a fine man."

Reider closed his eyes and breathed through his nose, a satisfied, beautiful breath, a breath of life.

Reider was the center of attention.

No one noticed as Lim pulled his 7.62-caliber Tokarev revolver from its holster. He reached slowly across his lower body and placed the muzzle gently on the back of Reider's left hand.

"Moi!" he screamed. "Animal!"

He pulled the trigger.

CHAPTER THIRTEEN

At that moment, in a certain office in Hanoi, the Political Officer responsible for Major Lim was considering Lim's dossier.

There was a problem.

Some of the facts were just that—facts—and indisputable. The Political Officer tried to sort them out in his mind, to make a mental pattern out of Lim's background . . .

Name: Lim, Phong Van

Religion: Born into Cao Dai faith; Baptised a

Roman Catholic, August, 1934.

Date and Place of Birth: Feb. 16, 1931, Ha Tay
Province, Village of Ha Don—15 kilometers SW of
Hanoi.

Height: 16.75 decimeters
Weight: 61 kilos
Complexion: Sallow
Hair: Black
Eyes: Dark Brown

Distinguishing Marks: Shrapnel scar, 15 decimeters above right nipple. 9mm bullet scar—entry
1 decimeter above inside left knee—exit scar jag-
ged, 125 decimeters, outer leg—no limp. Small,
dark mole on upper back (7th vertebra). Stiffness
of first meta-carpal, left hand (non-treated
Bennet's fracture).

SALIENT PARENTAL BACKGROUND

Father: Tich Thieu Lim, Born 1899 (?): died June,
1945. Tich Thieu Lim was a radical Vietnamese
born in Hanoi and steeped in the ideal of inde-
pendence and the Confucian ethic of filial piety.

As a young man, while a petty official of the
French Civil Service, Tich Thieu Lim worked
closely in the hierarchy of Ho Chi Minh. When
Minh, living in Canton, formed the Association of
Vietnamese Revolutionary Young Comrades (Viet
Nam Thonh Non Cach Mong Dong Chi Hay) refer-
red to generally as the Revolutionary Youth Asso-
ciation (RYA), Tich Thieu Lim deserted his clerical
post to assist. In 1926 he and his wife went to
China. He assisted the Central Committee with the

work of the "Revolutionary Educations" of 256
Vietnamese who would later return to organize
the nationwide "call system."

In 1931, the failing health of his pregnant wife (a
distant cousin of General Le Van Vien, leader of
the Binh Xuyen, who controlled both vice and
police in Saigon under an arrangement with the
French and later with Bao Dai) caused Tich Thieu
Lim to return to Hanoi. There he assisted with
fund raising activities.

When his wife died giving birth to their only
child (the subject), Tich Thieu was inconsolable. In
1933, when en route to Moscow, Ho Chi Minh,
after a vital, final briefing on the financial situation, took a personal interest in the plight of Tich
Thieu Lim and infant son. The baby was sent to
trusted party agents in France for immediate—
and if necessary, permanent—tending while the
father's valiant and invaluable work for his
country should continue.

Tich Thieu Lim was killed in June, 1945 by Japanese riflemen. He was assisting in the evacuation
of three American pilots along the Ho Chi Minh
trail.

A PROFILE OF PHONG VAN LIM

Educated: The Sorbonne.

Languages: Fluency in Vietnamese, French, and
English—passable in Spanish, Italian, and
German. Hobbies and interests: Savate, chess,
hand guns, and cooking.

Sent to France as a child and fostered by the

Ayme family (Party members) in Auxerre, France.
Spent two years in the United States; attended
classes at UCLA; no degree. At age 26, returned to
Vietnam. Dien Bien Phu had fallen and the Geneva
Accords had given international identity to a
divided Vietnam—The Republic of Vietnam
(South) and the Democratic Republic of Vietnam
(North of the 17th parallel).

Lim was bitter over the partition; only the vic-
torious Viet Minh were losers.

Lim was incredulous: How could the astute Ho
Chi Minh agree to such an agreement, based on the
flimsy hope for a national election? The south was
not even a signatory to the agreement.

Lim's hope for identity and purpose lay in what
he knew would be the thorn in the side of the
South's Diem government—the dormant, but
intact, organization of the NLF. It was this organization which, he knew, would be for the Viet Cong
(Vietnamese Communists) what "spirit" was for
the Viet Minh. He would help grow and sharpen
this thorn against the time it would serve as knife.

Arriving in Hanoi, Lim was met by close former
friends of his father. It was agreed he should infiltrate the South and become part of the apparatus; his aristrocratic blood and French education
would make him a very well-received orphan who
had found his way "home."

With assistance from his deceased mother's con-
tacts with the Binh Xuyen, he was quickly introduced into the inner circles of Saigon. Commis-
sioned as a first lieutenant in the ARVN, he was
attached to the country's only Airborne Brigade

(billeted in Saigon) as an intelligence officer. He served for two years with distinction. During this time he worked simultaneously to organize the NLF program aimed at destroying the South's armed forces from within—the deadly "Binh Van." In addition to chiseling away at the effectiveness of the individual ARVN soldier by means which often included pressure on the soldier's family, it developed and set policy for the handling of POW's (later amended to include captured Americans).

Mentioned in various dispatches on both sides of the 17th parallel for competence and valor, Phong Van Lim was promoted to captain in the ARVN on orders dated December 14, 1959. General Giap himself made him a covert captain in the NVA on the same date.)

That night Lim decided to get drunk—on a decadent "night on the town."

He met Ma Chi Ngai . . .

The Political Officer lit a cigarette, pushed himself back from the desk, drew the smoke into his lungs, and thought. Women he understood. And politics. Even religion, though it was hard to see how that could affect a party member one way or other.

But something had begun for Lim that night he met Ma Chi Mgai—some cause, some force, some power that still existed. Perhaps it could be that here the problem was? Was Lim inherently unstable? What exactly had been triggered in Lim by that initial meeting with Ma Chi Ngai?

CHAPTER FOURTEEN

The morphine was beginning to wear off. As it did, Lim knew, there would be the sharp, intense, unbearable pain—but there would also be a heightening of his mind's ability to function; there would be a clarity of mental power; there would come an exhilarating boost that would make him temporarily a superman. He had experienced it before. He knew what to expect.

Ma Chi Ngai . . .

He looked forward to the ecstasy of mental clar-

ity. It was worth the pain to achieve that purity of
consciousness. Pain. Purity. Perhaps there was
something to religion after all. First the sacrifice,
then the exultation.

Ma Chi Ngai . . .

The name secured itself within an inward
bunker of thought, oblivious to any world outside.

Ma Chi Ngai . . .

The name sounded in the very citadel of his being.

Ma Chi Ngai . . .

And then, through some quirk of the morphine,
the world dissolved into time and again it was that
night, a heaven and a hell ago . . .

He was not quite drunk. He was at that point
where the warm and lovely night around him im-
perceptibly blended with his brain. Almost. Not
quite. No doubt the stone of the cathedral ahead
was pure spun sugar; was not the Caucasian God a
great petit-four frosted in gray loaf cathedrals?
Mais, oui, M'sieu. C'est vrai. C'est indispu—indisputable, Sir. Indisputable. God, how barbaric the
speech of the American bastards. Indisputable. No
knowledge of how the cigarette came to be in his
hand. He pulled the smoke deep into his lungs.
Lucky Strike. Bon. Bon, mon ami.

Saigon. The Caucasians called it "the Paris of
the East." Ah, M'sieu, you do not know mon
Paris. . . . He felt very French. He paused at the
corner. He knew where he was . . .

Je suis dans la Rue Tudo—Freedom Street. It
had been Catinot, of course, but the French had

renamed it after the ship that brought their army to the city. Appropriate. Did not Tudo Street most typify the French influence? Rape my country and change her name. Make harlots of her avenues. . . .

Merde! Bullshit, as the Americans would say. Am I not as French as any of them?

Peut-être, M'sieu. The cigarette between his fingers was American. But the brandy in his gut was a very good Armagnac from the Gascon country, from the home of D'Artagnan. Lim smiled, pleased to link himself to the musketeer.

He had started the evening at the Saigon River docks. The night had been all warm magic and French dreams . . . beauty with texture. With the brandy warming his soul he had walked the avenues, letting the night traffic of the city and its sensuous beauty warm him. Paris of the East, yes. Tamarind trees, like women of the evening, lined the avenue, hidden by the night's gentle darkness; sidewalk cafes, exquisite import shops, fine night clubs—it all had a beautiful Gallic sense of fitness. Paris? No. Nevertheless, an acceptable facsimile.

He felt very French.

And warmed by more than brandy.

It was at this moment he became deeply aware of the cathedral looming up ahead, a gray shadow on the night as menacing as the possibility that God Himself was real. Ah!

The cathedral was no longer a gray loaf of spun sugar; its massive stone bulk stood athwart the night like the impregnable breastworks of the commander of the universe. Memory stirred in

Lim. That first sight of the cathedral at Auxerre . . .
thirteenth-century Gothic. Was there a European
God before the time of the soaring stone cathedrals? He had been, after all, a stranger in
France. . . .

"By the waters of Babylon we lay down; yea, we
wept as we remembered Zion. . . ."

Something dark and implacable, something
without form or meaning, reached out from the
cathedral to Lim. His steps grew heavy. He turned
into the cathedral.

Inside the bunker of God, the Saigon outside no
longer existed, and the creation of time was an-
nulled; there was only forever. Place, too. Lim had
the feeling he was neither in Saigon nor in Auxerre
—but in all cathedrals everywhere. The candles
that burned here had burned forever; the statues
of the saints lived their motionless stone lives; in
the shadowed heights of the cathedral ceiling, the
red symbol of the Holy Spirit burned like the
blood of God. Burn. Burn. Burn. How odd that the
timeless stone should burn with the presence of
Deity.

Without thinking, Lim genuflected, entered a
pew, and knelt on the smooth-worn mahogany rail.
He was back in his childhood, back in the timeless
embrace of this God who was neither the God of
his ancestors nor the God of his politics.

He considered his two military roles, considered the magnificent street that had brought his two
worlds together, and considered the consequences
to him of both. Now thoroughly sober, on his

knees, he was about to whisper his views to this God Who was obviously present.

But he thought, suddenly; better to get really drunk! and leaped from the pew.

The church was nearly deserted, yes. But there was a woman coming down the aisle, and, when he left the pew so precipitously, he fell full against her in the aisle.

"Pardonnez-moi, Madame." The apology was perfunctory. He intended to brush past her—as he would brush past anything inanimate or living, that got in his way.

But then he saw her face.

No, that was not what he saw. What he saw was not only this woman herself, but also a past and a future, a fulfillment of dreams, and something more: a symbol somehow enormously important to him but with a meaning that eluded him completely. The dark eyes were windows to a secret paradise—yet they combined a teasing, courtesan amusement with the naive surprise of a virginal girl. And the lips—holy as the perfumed breath of God—yet sensuous as the Saigon night outside. He was aware that the body inside the expensive cheongsam would, if he allowed his eyes to focus on it, wipe any cathedral inhibitions he might still have from his mind—he would have her on the altar itself, this night, this moment, and neither man, nor the Church, nor God Himself would stop him.

He was utterly stunned by the intensity of his emotions, and he recoiled from them completely, taking refuge, as any proper mandarin would, in extreme formality.

So excuses came quickly, too loud, embarrassing to them both. Escorting her out the door, he allowed himself to look deep into her dark eyes before making a composed apology. That one look, in the diffused romantic light of the night on the steps of the cathedral of God, struck something deeper and tenderer in his soul than had any of his earlier involvement with the Caucasian God, and, as the formal apology gently left his lips, he stood momentarily mute before this soft new goddess in the pale blue gown.

Yet . . . he was not entirely captured.

At the perimeter of his mind certain vague thoughts probed like exploratory patrols. . . .

When he collided with her, she had been coming down the aisle into the church—yet she had left with him. And she had apologized as quickly as he, like him had been too loud, too embarrassing. . . .

So . . . nevertheless. . . . He saluted smartly and left abruptly.

He was two blocks down the avenue before it occurred to him that he did not know her name.

The first bar he found was his last. From there, at three in the morning, three men of the Brigade carried him to a CV Renault taxi. He was singing— in French—"Under the Bridges of Paris."

It was the first night he had been drunk in ten years.

The next day Captain Lim was at the cathedral at dusk.

The woman did not come.

Not that day, nor the next.

Nor the day after that.

But the following day she came—and after that there was never to be a day for the rest of his life that he would not think of her at least once.

No, it was not "Madame," but "Mademoiselle." The name was Ma Chi Ngai. She was as beautiful as he had remembered her being.

Yet there was one strange thing. Lim's first desire should have been to go to bed with her. After all. . . . But with Ma Chi Ngai it was like being in the presence of a virginal goddess pedestaled on an altar of purity.

Which created all kinds of problems.

When another officer in the Brigade would brag about the piece of tail he had had the night before, Lim would boil with inner rage, murderous fury only barely controlled. He knew it was totally irrational—yet he could not help himself. It was bad enough when the officer was Vietnamese; he lived in fear that one day he would look into the face of an American bragging about the piece of Viet ass he had—and would go completely berserk.

The other side of the coin, of course, was the fact that the more virginal, the more chaste, the more unapproachable Ma Chi Ngai was, the more he wanted her.

And to compound the problem, he was intuitively aware that she wanted him, too.

There were times when Lim was almost persuaded that the Caucasian God really did exist—

and that He was a total sadist, thoroughly enjoying torturing Lim and Ma Chi. But there were other times when Lim dreamed of the moment the two would come together, the moment the perfumed beds of Paradise would be theirs.

So he alternated between feeling like a foolish schoolboy and feeling like a damn fool man with irrational inhibitions. In the meantime, though, he and Ma Chi spent every available moment together. She showed him Saigon—and whatever part of the countryside was available to them; through her eyes he began to see his native land more deeply, to see what it had been, to see what it might be. She was his eyes, and it did not matter for the moment that the Vietnam he was seeing ran counter to Marxist-Leninist thought. After all, it did not fit American—or French—thought either. Like so many before him, Lim—who thoroughly enjoyed the *Rubaiyat*—had divorced old barren politics from his bed and taken the daughter of passion to his wife. Neither the God of Moses nor the dialectical inevitability of Marx mattered; he gladly shoved them both aside for Ma Chi.

But three into two won't go. A Vestal virgin, a warrior, and abstinence create one hell of a discontinuity in any Creator's world.

So there came an afternoon, around four o'clock, when abstinence was destroyed. . . .

After that, of course, the days were pure joy.

Perhaps every man needs to live at the top of the mountain at least once in his life—and for Lim these were the days on the mountain, the days, as the American song said, of wine and roses. There was total contentment merely in being in the presence of Ma Chi; there was total ecstasy in the other meaning of being on the mountain—Ma Chi was very, very good at love. . . .

CHAPTER FIFTEEN

The Political Officer's dossier on Ma Chi Ngai did not contain the same information as Lim's memory. Nor would the PO have cared; he was concerned only with matters relevant to Marxist-Leninist agitprop needs.

The affair had resulted—initially—in only minor loss of effectiveness in Comrade Lim.

With the election of President John F. Kennedy in the United States, aid to South Vietnam rapidly increased, stepping up to an estimated 1.2 million dollars a day. The romantic new president, a fan of novelist Ian Fleming, took a special interest in the flamboyant Special Warfare Center at Fort Bragg, North Carolina, and this intensified the foreign officer exchange program with that country.

As a distinguished junior officer of diversified background and superior education, Captain Lim, intelligence officer of his nation's only Airborne Brigade, was a prime candidate for "exchange." For reasons of clandestine priorities as well as personal motives—Ma Chi Ngai—he postponed the inevitable as long as he could. It was the NLF which finally decided and made him go.

In September, 1961, Captain Lim arrived at Fort Bragg. Nine months later he received a special commendation and a certificate as a "distinguished graduate" of his class.

But Lim's life was falling apart.

For six months prior to his return, there had been no response from Ma Chi to his letters. When he returned to Saigon, she was not to be found. It took several of the best operatives from the Binh Xuyen to locate her—in the Don Konh Hotel in Cholon, the Chinese section of Saigon.

The message came cryptically by telephone to Lim's office in Brigade HQ. Without a word or a by-your-leave, he commandeered the first jeep he saw and drove through the jumble of traffic like the temporary madman the news had made him.

The Political Officer lit another cigarette. He felt a momentary twinge of guilt from such prodigal use of tobacco, but there was this matter of Comrade Lim.

Why had the business meant so much to Lim? Surely Lim had understood what American money could do. What did he expect?

The PO wished he could see the matter through Lim's eyes. . . .

Through the euphoria of the fading morphine, warm images of Ma Chi Ngai floated through Lim's brain only to disappear instantly in a sudden shock of unbearable agony from his amputated arm. He fell immediately into total unconsciousness.

When he came to, the images in his brain were gray monotones, stark, his memories jerking him directly to the Don Konh Hotel. . . .

When he came in the door, the bar was just opening. A few of the girls were in a corner of the empty dance floor, sitting on straight-back chairs. The barmaid was drying glasses, and a lone American corporal sat staring into his beer glass. Lim grabbed the first girl in full stride. Pulling her up by the hair with one hand, he gripped her throat viciously with the other and growled Ma Chi's name. The prostitute choked an answer he did not hear. He relaxed his grip slightly and asked again —with more menace. The girl coughed a room number two floors below. Dropping her like a dead fish, Lim took the four reversed flights of stairs in two bounds per landing, ran the deserted corridor and kicked down the thin door. He fired once. The top of the nude American's head splatted against the bedpost.

The image of Ma Chi momentarily refused to focus.

After all, he had spent years in France, months in America; there was this understanding of Western attitudes . . . humiliation . . . intuitively he knew that the particular activity—

But the image of Ma Chi that did focus was of her lying on her back, full length, nude, eyes deep pools of darkness.

Diagonally, across the bed, Lim sighted the automatic precisely on the pupil of her right eye. First the right. Then the left. He had seen his motherland through her eyes; he would close the vision forever.

She did not move.

The image changed.

Color.

Flesh and blood.

The living woman.

The blood of the dead American, like the blood of a slaughtered animal, was reaching for her as though it were a surrealist red glove.

Through her eyes.

No. It was finished. There was nothing more to see. The dream would remain with him forever, coming back each day; the reality no longer existed.

Lim threw the loaded automatic toward her. It landed on her navel, bounced and lay still, muzzle against her left breast, handle pointing ironically toward the brush at the junction of her thighs.

He turned his back on her and walked out the door.

But Lim had not gone two steps from the open

door when the dark, sullen cheapness of the hall began to act on him.

He had been hating the American—hating him for taking Ma Chi to this place, taking her here as though she were a common prostitute, taking her here so many times that even the harlots of the hotel knew her very name. He had paid the American—blasted the Caucasian animal's brains.

But Ma Chi—should she suffer?

The cultures within him—French, Viet, American—fought to claim Lim's consciousness.

He slammed his fist into the dirty wall of the corridor; the hall reverberated with the crash, and the hotel grew silent—silent as a cage of animals suddenly invaded. He went back in the room.

She lay exactly as he had left her.

He went over to the left side of the bed and picked up the Walther; the tips of his fingers touched momentarily the flesh just below her navel; he blocked completely out of his mind the thought that came to him.

For a moment shorter than it would have taken a grenade to explode he looked deep into her eyes and saw—as he holstered the Walther—hope rise out of the depths like the coming of dawn in the dark jungle morning. Unspoken, the thought in her mind came across as clearly as though she had shouted.

Silently, in his soul, he cursed all the gods—but the look in her eyes—and the memories—did bring forth from him one small act of compassion: his right hand chopped down against the side of her head so quickly she was unconscious before she knew what had hit her.

Then he proceded to do what he had to do.

The French, in their Revolution, their struggle for liberation—had bound nude nuns and priests together and thrown them in the Seine. The English had enshrined in their literary pantheon the albatross around the neck of the sinning Ancient Mariner. The Americans were sex-crazy. His own Viet people—

Lim stood by the bed. The emotion had drained out of him. Emotions. Damn all emotions. Neither Marx nor Lenin would approve emotions. I am a soldier in the struggle for liberation. There must be an example. . . .

He tore a bedsheet into strips and made ropes, ropes liberally soaked in the blood of the dead American. He pulled the dead American over on the unconscious Ma Chi, and then he tied the corpse to her.

The touch of her living flesh burned him like napalm.

She was beginning to stir just before he went out the door. The first scream came when he was halfway down the hall.

The screams grew louder, louder, louder. . . .

Lim disappeared back into the LLDB, attempting to lose himself in work, devoting all his energies to it. But now he knew that he would not be able to maintain the facade very much longer. It nauseated him to smile and play the ignorant peasant for the Americans.

There was no complaint lodged against him for the killing. Ma Chi Ngai was just another whore who had gotten herself in trouble, and the Americans didn't want any stink about one of their rosy-cheeked young boys being terminated under such conditions. The matter was lost in the files of the Criminal Investigation Division, and that was that.

Only in Hanoi was the full story known. It was regrettable that a prized agent had so nearly lost his head over a worthless woman, but the incident had its usefulness; it gave them even more reason to be certain of Lim's loyalty. If ever he became a problem, he could just be turned over to the civilian police for the murder. In all likelihood he would never compromise his comrades, believing that the party was still as loyal to him as he was to it.

It was three years later that they decided to activate him and engineer the takeover of Plei Jrong, with the promise of promotion to major once the camp was taken. They knew how to handle Lim. His weaknesses and strengths were each used to make him of more value to the party. Instead of being admonished by his superiors, he was quietly praised, reassured of the understanding of the party and its concern for his welfare. The party had become his Church, which would forgive and punish transgressors according to their merits.

The party was forgiving, and it had forgiven Lim. It had presented him with a new opportunity —batallion commander of an NVA regimental combat team.

The Political Officer's cigarette had that unpleasant taste that comes from a half-smoked
stub.

Problem?

Probably not.

Major Lim was a very good man.

As long as his fears and weaknesses were
understood.

CHAPTER SIXTEEN

Movement awakened Reider. He was on a make-shift stretcher, his leg wrapped in tattered rags and bound tightly. His left hand throbbed, burned. Didn't feel right. He wanted to look at it, but he didn't have the strength to raise it. He watched the jungle drifting by overhead; the stretcher swayed between two VC soldiers. He drifted to sleep, and was jarred awake by the high-pitched chatter of voices. The stretcher tipped, and he was dumped on the floor of a hut. One of the VC rolled back a mat in one corner of the hut and disappeared through the floor. Two others picked Reider up, dragged him over to the corner and slid him down a dark, dirty tunnel. At the bottom it was light, and the two VC picked him up again and carried him past stacks of automatic weapons and hurrying soldiers. At the end of the tunnel, the two soldiers slapped him against the dirt wall. All he could remember later was the light overhead staring him in the eyes, the stench of medicine, and screaming.

The light and the heat began to work on Reider. Another time, another war. Korea—cold. Cold or hot, one or the other, always extremes. Inchon. The Chosun reservoir. Vague, uneasy images flashed around the perimeter of his consciousness. Sometimes they marched to the beat of some unseen, eternal drum . . . rat-tat-tat, rat-tat-tat, rat-tat-tat . . . in hell, or nowhere. Sometimes the images were completely silent, like the soundless flashes of the perimeter of a firefight remembered in a nightmare . . . far off and long ago . . . Sometimes they were real things . . . Long, cold nights and fear of sleeping bags . . . How many men had died in their bags because the zippers froze? Korea. Two years, some days! What difference? I learned my trade there. Memories. Good ones. Bad ones. What difference? Japan. Camp Zama. Japanese hot baths. Tarzan movies with Tarzan speaking Japanese. Well, why not? The Ginza in Tokyo, doll-like little bar girls. "Hi, Joe. I love too much you buy whiskey Coke. Dai jobu. Okay, Number One skivvy honcho." . . . Civvy time discharge.

Coming up short-timer. Gonna get out and make a
mint . . .

Reider slept.

When he awoke there was no sharp dividing line
between the images and the reality. There was
only the light overhead, merely another image,
and the distant aching throb in his hand. He closed
his eyes and took up where he had left off.

Only this time the images were mostly connected . . .

Gonna make it big in civvy life. Damn right. I'm
too smart to be a lifer in the Army . . . But that
wasn't the way it worked out. There was little
work for ex-soldiers, and what he did find didn't
satisfy him. Something was missing. A sense of be-
longing was gone. In the service, there had been a
feeling of oneness and purpose.

After four months, one fall morning in Sacra-
mento, he found himself in front of the recruiter's
window. Why the hell not? Reider entered. The
sergeant at the desk raised his eyes and smiled
slowly. Without a word, he took out the necessary
forms, ready to send Reider back where he belonged. Reider nodded and began to fill in the
blanks . . . Rat-tat-tat. March to the drums. . . .

When Reider finished, the recruiter looked the
papers over, and spoke for the first time. "You
with the 173rd Airborne? That was a raunchy
group of outlaws. I was with the Eighty Deuce till
they gave me this desk. There's one outfit you
should think about, Reider, my boy. That's the
77th Special Service Force. It's one hell of a group

of men. All pros. All volunteers. They're going to
be expanding into a larger force, so this would be
a good time for you to walk in. You got the quali-
fications. Want to try it?"

Reider nodded his head, and the recruiter made
an entry on the forms. He turned them over to
Reider, who didn't read them, just signed his
name. The recruiting sergeant took the forms
back, stood up and put out his hand.

"Welcome home, soldier. Welcome home."

Reider opened his eyes wide, but the dream lin-
gered with him a little longer. The recruiter had
been right. Home was the service. It could never
be replaced by a woman, any woman. She had
never really mattered to him. That's where the
guilt came from. He had been a user always, never
giving anything of himself, at least not the part of
him she wanted. The part that would be there
when she was lonely or wanted to be held and
talked to. It was clear now. There was never anything he could have done about it. The part of him
she wanted just wasn't there, didn't exist. You
can't give what you don't have, even if you want
too. All you can do is fake it for a time, because
failure of any kind is too hard to admit to yourself.
In some ways he felt closer to Lim than he ever
had to her. He and Lim had something in common.

He tried to summon up his wife's face. It
wouldn't come; he found only a hazy blur that
faded away and was gone back to the past, where
she belonged. It was good. As she faded, so did his
guilt.

For ten minutes he tested his vision, moving his eyes from side to side, looking at the room and the bed and the guard at the doorway. His face felt almost normal, although raised rough scabs ran along the chin line and on his cheeks. He was glad there was no mirror in the room. Raising his right hand, he touched the bandages around his left. There was something obviously different about it. That was plain, even under the thick gauze bandages that encased it. Then it hit him. That dirty son of a bitch shot off the middle finger. Once he had remembered what was wrong, it didn't seem to matter much any more. It was just a finger. Hell, most demo men were missing at least one. It could have been a lot worse. He fell asleep again. When he awoke, he was hungry; some time later, he didn't know when, an orderly came in with a bowl of cold rice with bits of fishhead and pumpkin mixed in. He ate, and quickly downed the tea brought to him. For a short while warmth came to him, and he began to feel better. Then the hunger came again, and he slept.

He did not know how many times he slept or how many times the silent, small man brought the rice bowl and the bits of meat. It could have been only a day or two, or it could have been two weeks, since that day in the jungle when Kosun had died.

When he finally was able to stay awake for an entire day, they moved him. Two VC guards, with AK-47 assault rifles, and two hospital orderlies put him on a stretcher and took him from the room. A medical attendant sat behind a desk. Twenty feet away, a guard was standing in front of a set of doors that led into another tunnel. They took him in and left him there.

On the second day of his stay in the tunnel, he was lying with his head to the wall, his arm propped up under his chin, when a voice spoke behind him.

"Dreaming of home, Sergeant?"

Reider jerked his head around. Lim was leaning against the edge of his bed, the stump of his arm bandaged.

"I'm happy to see there is some life in you, Sergeant. Last time I saw you, I thought perhaps I had lost my esteemed prisoner. Are you able to sit up? Good. If you can walk, I would like for you to see what we have here. You know, you really owe me a great deal, sergeant. I had much trouble convincing the medical people here that you, a mere NCO, were a very important political prisoner. Especially a prisoner who required so much of their time and medical supplies. But enough of this talk."

Reider had no desire to get up, but he knew he needed exercise. Walking would help strengthen his legs so he could escape. "All right, Lim," he said.

A guard came up the tunnel and jerked Reider to his feet. They walked him down to a room off a side corridor and showed him a pile of clothing on the bed.

"Dress yourself, Sergeant," Lim instructed.

Reider put on the clothes—American fatigues.

The feel of boots on his feet again was pleasant.

"Hurry up, Sergeant," Lim urged him.

Reider, the guard, and Lim walked down the tunnel past the guards on duty. As they walked, Lim began a running monologue, "This is one of our better field hospitals, Sergeant. And it will interest you to know we are very, very close to Saigon. We came by truck on one of our jungle roads. We're in what you refer to as War Zone Delta. I am sure your American intelligence apparatus has told you this entire area is secured, and no doubt it is. As you can see, we have secured it," Lim sniggered. "Right under the nose of your ARVN associates."

"Tell them about it," said Reider. "Why keep it a secret?"

"Such hostility," said Lim. "And after I have saved your life. Are you not grateful that I didn't take more from you than just one small digit?"

"I'm grateful you've let me live to express my appreciation, Lim."

"Reider, you amaze me. Perhaps you think you will escape. I think not. You are mine, Sergeant, to do with as I please."

"Shit," said Reider.

"Be quiet, now," said Lim. "Talking for you is so much a waste of words, especially in view of your —how shall I say it?—your position. But I have good news for you. Our doctors tell me you soon will be fit to travel. In a few days we shall take you from this confined life underground, and you will start to live a life among our people. You will learn to appreciate the beauty of our great country."

Lim turned into another corridor. It was stacked from floor to ceiling with medical supplies. A few of the boxes were inscribed with Vietnamese characters, a few appeared to be Chinese, and one particularly large box had Russian characters on it. But most of the packing crates were stenciled "U.S. ARMY MEDICAL SUPPLIES."

"Now, Sergeant, you will see how our Special Delivery system works. These medicines so thoughtfully prepared and provided to you by the People's Army of Liberation were given to us by some of your friends in Saigon—the grateful South Vietnamese allies whom your propaganda experts would have the world believe are only interested in the good of their country. But you see, Reider, those wonderful allies are also businessmen, and like many businessmen—perhaps things are the same in your country—they are interested in the amount of money that changes hands, particularly into their hands. I am amazed by the patriotism shown by your friends in South Vietnam. It is quite a collection of supplies, is it not?

Reider thought of all the Americans who had died fighting the North Vietnamese and the Viet Cong who were being helped by supplies stolen from his own army by the very people the Americans were supposed to be helping. But that was the way of it, he knew. A reality of Nam. He also knew that if Charley won this war, the first ones to go under the ax would be those selfsame profiteers. Communists were very practical about some matters: those who had sold out the South Vietnamese for money would likely do the same to them once they were in power.

"You are silent, Sergeant," Lim taunted him.

"There are traitors in all wars, Lim," Reider replied. "And these people in Saigon who are selling our supplies on the black market aren't any different from those who sold arms and supplies to the enemy of any other time. It doesn't surprise me."

"You know, Sergeant, the more I am around you, the more I like you. Some of the prisoners I have interrogated, some of your comrades, were very arrogant. You are arrogant, too, but you have a professional's attitude, Sergeant, and that is good, because that is what I am—a professional. And even though you have caused me to lose the use of my arm, and you have wiped out my patrol, I have a certain amount of regard for you, Sergeant."

"Thanks," said Reider.

They passed more guards and entered a large room with a ceiling perhaps twelve feet high. Reider estimated the room to be thirty or forty feet long, and thirty feet wide. The floor was dirt and the roof had been shored with wooden beams. Stacked along the walls were piles of black pajamas and woven straw baskets. The entire center of the space was crowded with bicycles.

"This, Sergeant," said Lim, "is our motor pool. You find it amusing? These bicycles with their straw baskets can carry nearly two hundred pounds of rice, a box of hand grenades, or a box of ammunition. If we used trucks, as your own army does, perhaps we would be more vulnerable to your airplanes. I once saw one of your fast fighter planes try to strafe a bicycle. And do you know, Sergeant, it does not work too well. A bicycle is no target for an aircraft. It is easy to hide and hard to hit. And with our much simpler, more practical, and much less expensive equipment, we move more in one night than your Army Transport Command does in two days. What do you think of that?"

"I think you're afraid of those airplanes, Lim. I think you're afraid of the choppers, and I think you're afraid of the bombs."

"Sergeant, you annoy me. You are more obstinate than intelligent. All the power and all the money cannot conquer what you cannot find to fight. I have one more thing to show you."

Lim led him along another corridor, through another set of doors, and into an even larger room filled with cases of American cigarettes. Stacked in the center of the room were twenty cases of green canisters with white English lettering.

"Smoke bombs," said Reider. "How did you get those?"

"We bought them," Lim replied. "Imagine, Sergeant, the surprise of your helicopter pilots when they are directed to land by the smoke and find the People's Army of Liberation there to meet them on the ground. I have seen some of those pilots; one I remember well. I killed him. Such a simple trick."

Reider imagined the chopper coming down, the gunners in the doors ready, but relaxed, sure they were landing in support of a South Vietnamese force. He could see the fear on their faces as the bullets ripped into the chopper and the tracers rising from the trees hit the rotors. He knew now why so many choppers had failed to return from missions in the last four months. He had information now that was needed in Saigon.

"And now, Sergeant," said Lim, "your guard will assist you. You must go back to your bed and rest."

Lim spoke to the guard in Viet, and the guard shoved Reider back down the corridor and marched him to his bed and pushed him onto it. Then two more guards came to handcuff and chain him to the framework of the bed. It was a sure sign he was getting better, Reider thought.

Two days later, after the little man had left Reider his bowl of rice and bits of meat, Lim came in.

"As soon as you have eaten, Sergeant," said Lim, "I have a small gift for you. Please inform the guard when you have finished."

When Reider had eaten, the guard removed the bowl and returned with two more guards and Major Lim. One of the guards carried an old-fashioned yoke and a large roll of white adhesive tape. Lim spoke to the guards in Viet, and they started to put the yoke on Reider. He struggled but was swiftly subdued.

"It would be wise to submit," said Lim. "My men have orders to kill if you resist too strenuously. It is good to see you have recovered some of that fine American strength."

Lim took the roll of tape from one of the guards and placed it between his bandaged stump and his body, holding it there while he tried to pull a strip from the roll. After a number of unsuccessful attempts, he gave the tape back to the guard. Lim's eyes narrowed at Reider as he growled, "You see, don't you, Sergeant, that I have some difficulty with the arm you removed. Do not turn your head! Hold still! I do not intend to give you an opportunity to yell. That is a habit of yours that I do not like."

"I'm not crazy about some of yours," Reider snapped.

Lim smiled. "We have a long journey ahead of us tonight. It will be easier for you if you adjust to your equipment before we leave."

Reider shook free of the guards and stood with his back against the wall, trying to project his hatred with his eyes. Lim stepped back and made a mocking bow. One of the guards ripped off a strip of tape and sealed Reider's mouth while the second guard held him fast.

"Until tonight, Sergeant," said Lim, as he turned away.

Reider tried to sleep, but the yoke made it impossible for him to relax. Finally, he sat on the edge of the bed, resting the yoke against the wall, and late in the afternoon he managed to doze for fifteen or twenty minutes.

Lim and five guards came for him early in the evening, led him through the network of tunnels and up through the floor of the hut he vaguely remembered having left earlier. There were numerous other VC waiting at the doorway. As they left the village, they were joined by twenty more black-pajama-clad troops armed with submachineguns. Reider thought they were marching west.

At dawn they halted beside a river. Reider leaned against a tree, exhausted, torn and scratched from the long trek through the jungle, trying to rest the heavy yoke against anything that would relieve its pressure on his shoulders. As the day lightened, a village took shape on the other side of the river and beyond it, another village, partially obscured by camouflage netting and brush, with sentries patrolling underneath the netting. The first village appeared lackadaisical.

Lim edged over to Reider and said, "You may remember this river. We were near here once, some time ago. Soon you will be in your new home; we must find suitable quarters for you there."

Lim bowed mockingly to Reider and then returned to his men and led them to the edge of the river, where they moved the brush hiding several small rafts. Launching the rafts into the muddy water, they crossed, swinging with the current and nosing softly onto the other bank, twenty to thirty yards down the river from the village. Lim and his men moved the rafts into the brush and

used branches to eliminate all traces of the tracks
on the beach. They then bypassed the first village
and assembled beneath the camouflage netting of
the second compound. As sentries saluted Lim,
Reider was shoved toward a crudely fashioned
stockade. One of the guards there made a move to
remove the yoke, but Lim yelled a curt, "No!"
Reider was thrown against the gate of the enclosure.

"Forgive him, Sergeant," said Lim. "He was
about to remove your collar. It was so thoughtless
of him. I think since you are just out of hospital, it
would be better to leave the yoke on to protect you
from the cold."

Reider stared at the smiling, moon-faced major.
"It's easy to see you're always thinking of me,
Major."

"Sergeant, your stubborness makes the task of
reeducating you much more pleasurable."

Lim then bowed deeply in mock politeness and
gave an order to the guards. Reider was pushed
through the gate of the enclosure, and he hit the
ground inside, sliding on the yoke. His shoulder
felt as though it had been wounded. He lay there
for a moment and heard the gate of the compound
swing closed, while Lim rattled off orders to the
sentries outside.

The morning light filtered through the thatched
roof and bamboo walls of the stockade. Reider lifted his head slowly, and then sat up and moved
back against the wall to rest the yoke against the
bamboo.

A Montagnard lay against the opposite wall, his stocky frame reduced by emaciation—a skeleton of a man with hollow cheeks and thin, dirty arms with tendons drawn like piano wire. At the opposite end of the stockade was a crude wooden cross with a Vietnamese tied to it upside down, hanging very still. The discipline Simon Peter, had been crucified upside down. Reider remembered. Three other men sat near the end of the enclosure.

Reider's mind turned to thoughts of escape. He would never resign himself to his fate until he had wasted away. He had said it before; there were worse things than being dead. That was his ace in the hole, his road to freedom if all else failed.

CHAPTER SEVENTEEN

The three men at the far end stared at Reider for perhaps ten minutes. Then one rose slowly, as if he were very weak, and stumbled across the dirt to sit down beside Reider. "Need some help?" he asked.

Reider rose to his knees. "No, I'm okay."

The other man sat down. "You American?"

"Yes."

"Well, it's not much of a spot you picked to land in. My name's Meder, John Meder. I'm a leftenant in the Australian forces. You can call me Aussie, if you like; most of the men here do. The other two there are Yanks. The guy on the left is a chopper pilot; the other is a navigator, he's in pretty bad shape. His name's Bill Sutherland. Pilot's name is Clint McGann."

"Reider, Special Forces. You'll have to excuse me for not shaking hands."

Reider and the Australian crossed the compound and sat down near the others. The one called McGann reached over as if to help make Reider more comfortable. Reider shook him off. Sutherland said nothing. "Who are the other two guys?" Reider asked Meder.

"Those two?" He nodded toward the Montagnard and the babbler. "We don't really know. They've been here so long I don't think they know who they are. The one up there on the cross is a villager who threw food to us when they were starving us for a while. He lasted four days, died this morning. They've really been at him."

"Look," said McGann, "you want us to try and take that thing off you?"

"The Charley that runs this camp is a strange one," said Meder. "Pretty well educated, I think; and he hates Americans like the very devil. He's been using that guy on the cross as a reminder to the villagers. Every morning before they go to work in the fields, and every night when they come back, he opens the gate and makes all of them take a good look."

"Then this isn't a Viet Cong village?"

"Nope," said McGann, "I don't think so. But the VC have them so scared, you can forget any ideas you might have about them helping us out. They're too scared."

"Seems to me at least one of them could get loose and get word out on what's going on," said Reider.

"Well," said McGann, "maybe you better take another look at the local boy who didn't do so well."

"There's one consolation," said the Australian. "The VC captain that's been running this village is being replaced by some regular major. Maybe things will get a little bit better around here."

Reider almost laughed. Then he lost control and laughed out loud. The others stared at him, thinking maybe he had gone around the bend already. Then he told them about Lim, and how he had been captured, and what had happened since then.

"You don't look in such good shape," said Meder. "How long ago were you captured?"

"I don't know," said Reider. "I haven't had a chance to look at a calendar. They kept me in the field hospital, I don't know, maybe a week, two weeks. It's hard to tell. Look, have you guys figured any way to get out of here yet?"

"Not much chance," said McGann, "unless we get some help from the outside. The village is a dodge. Choppers fly over every so often, but all they see is a peaceful village. Everybody's so scared over there that they won't make a move, and this camp's so covered over with camouflage netting it'd be nearly impossible to see anything from above. The best thing we can do is hope that a search and destroy patrol comes up through this area. But I'm not sure that will ever happen. I think maybe we're in Cambodia, and if we are, you know what that means. We're not going to get out, because nobody's going to come over the border and look for us."

Reider didn't tell him that wasn't true. He knew that if his people found out where he was, they'd make a try for him.

McGann continued, "My hunch is we're just on the other side of the border, because the VC captain is one cocksure commie. He never seems to worry too much."

"Still, though," said Meder, "the choppers do come over. Maybe we're still in South Vietnam."

"What about Sutherland?" Reider asked, lowering his voice. Sutherland had not moved since Reider had sat down. "Does he talk?"

"Not too much any more," said McGann. "He's in pretty bad shape. He talked back a few too many times. The captain put him on starvation rations two weeks ago. He's lost a lot of his fight. When we try to sneak some food to him the guards come in and take it all away. We've managed a couple of times, though."

"When do you get fed?"

"About noon," Meder said, "if they feel like it, but you never can tell. Sometimes they'll skip a day or so just to make us get really hungry. A lot of times they throw the food in over the top of the gate; they like to see us scramble for it in the dirt. The first couple of times they did that, I wouldn't scramble. But after your stomach starts to shrivel up, you'll do damn near anything to get some food, even if it's a lousy piece of rotten fish with dirt all over it. But I think if I ever get out of this rathole, I'm never going to look at rice again."

A little after noon, two guards entered the compound and put down three bowls of rice and one small bowl of meat for McGann, Meder, and Reider. Guards watched to make sure none of the food was shared with Sutherland. Reider ate slowly, carefully slipping bits of rice into his shirt pocket, holding his hand over his mouth so the guards could not see the rice fall. He managed to get a couple of bits of meat in his pocket, too. Reider noticed that McGann was doing the same.

When the guards had gone, they waited an hour to make sure no one was watching, and then they huddled around Sutherland, trying to get him to eat what they had saved. He was very weak and unable to hold any of his food in his hands. He had to be force-fed, and he seemed to have a hard time swallowing. His eyes were only half open, and he made no sound.

Late in the afternoon, a guard came inside, checked his watch, and threw open the gates. At a signal from the guard, a long file of Vietnamese walked with their eyes down toward the ground and filed in. They were herded together tightly in the gateway. Ten minutes later the Viet Cong captain entered, with Major Lim close behind him.

The captain began screaming in Vietnamese, pointing toward the man on the cross. One or two villagers answered, and the captain screamed in Vietnamese; this time they all answered. The captain pointed again to the man on the cross, spoke to the guards, and watched the villagers being marched out.

Lim studied Reider and nodded to him slightly, but did not cross the compound. Suddenly Lim and the VC captain turned and left. The silence of the night settled upon the compound.

At sunrise, Reider's back and arms were aflame from his effort to sleep with the yoke on him. A guard outside yelled in Vietnamese, and the gates were thrown open. Again the villagers were herded inside the stockade, followed by the VC captain and Major Lim. The captain again began screaming in Vietnamese and pointing to the man on the cross; the villagers again answered. Then the captain pointed toward Major Lim, and apparently introduced him to the crowd. Lim moved toward the villagers; the captain stepped aside with a little bow.

McGann whispered to Reider, "Is that your boy?"

"He's mine, all right," said Reider. "One fine day."

Lim, smiling, delivered a short but obviously threatening speech in Vietnamese, bowed to the crowd, and then bowed to the VC captain. The captain screamed a command, and the villagers were marched away. The guards closed the gate. Lim and the VC captain strolled toward Reider and the others. Sutherland was flat on his back, still semiconscious.

Lim stopped before them, and stood legs wide apart. "Well, Sergeant," he said, "you look very comfortable. And I see you have found some friends."

Reider rose. "I must introduce you, major," he said. "A regular army officer such as you is entitled to that formality. May I present Leftenant Meder and Captain McGann. The man lying down is Lieutenant Bill Sutherland. You liberators are starving him."

"Sergeant, you are very cute. Flippant, I think the word is. And you are in no position to be flippant, as you should be able to understand from looking at this . . . Sutherland. Don't worry, Sergeant, I will think of something very special for you, something worthy of a man like you. Sutherland was a weak man and without your will power. He was really quite easy, the captain tells me. But you—you will be different. But in the end, you will wish that I had done to you the kindness that was shown to Mr. Sutherland."

"You gutless piece of shit," Reider muttered. "That's what you are, Major. You are a. . . ."

Lim's hand caught him along the side of the head, and he fell heavily upon Sutherland, who was too weak to raise his arms and break the fall. McGann and Meder rushed to help him up as Lim stood over them, screaming, "Keep it up, Sergeant! Just keep it up! It makes the game that much more enjoyable for me. I'm happy to see you're too stupid to see that you can't win."

Reider got to his knees, swaying under the heavy yoke, and then he stood erect, faced Lim, and spat in his face.

"Dog!" Lim screamed as he struck Reider across the cheek with his fist. Reider went down, and Lim kicked him savagely on the legs and then around his ribs.

McGann tried to push the major away, but the VC captain knocked McGann aside, and joined Lim in kicking Reider. After a few moments, Lim seemed to regain some semblance of his composure, and he and the captain ceased working on Reider.

"Very well, Sergeant," Lim said breathing very hard, his eyes quite bright. "If you choose to behave like an animal, I will do my best to treat you like an animal."

He turned abruptly and, followed by the VC captain, left the compound. The two guards stared in at Reider as he lay face down, coughing blood into the dirt. They smiled briefly, and then locked the gates.

"Can you talk?" McGann asked.

Reider croaked, "Yes, I think so."

Meder said, "Hang on, I'm going to poke around and see if you've got a broken rib."

Meder's hands explored Reider's sides, pushing, moving. "Looks like you're lucky," said Meder. "No broken ribs. What the hell did you do that for?"

Reider smiled in reply.

"Listen, Reider," said McGann, "I wouldn't do that kind of thing if I were you. That bloody bastard's got it in for you. He's got it in for you good. Maybe you don't know this, but there ain't no way out of here, Reider. We're stuck. It's like I told you. Nobody's going to find us. And the only chance you've got of staying alive is keeping that son of a bitch off your back until the war's over. That is, if they don't kill us before then."

"Besides that," said Meder, "that major of yours may decide to take some of your brass out on Sutherland, and he can't take any more. I don't want to see him die just because you and your major have a feud going. We've been here over six months now, maybe longer, and it's a day-to-day ordeal just to survive; and I want to stay alive, Reider. I don't like to sound cowardly, but I'd like to live to leave here one of these days. Now why don't you leave your major alone? I'll get some water and clean you up."

Reider lay with his eyes closed. Meder crossed the compound and returned with a bowl of water, cleaning the cut that ran across his cheek, and daubed at his bloody lips with a dampened wad of his soiled shirt.

Reider slept for awhile, awoke at noon, talked to McGann and Meder, and tried to get some food into Sutherland, who now shook violently with chills.

At dawn the villagers came again, looking at the body on the cross. The smell was horrible now. A lot of villagers looked at Reider, squatting down in the dirt with the yoke on, his face badly bruised and puffy. Reider's body ached as he searched their faces for signs of encouragement—signs that one of these Vietnamese was partisan, that he was willing to get some word out. But Reider's eyes encountered only vacant stares, and an occasional glint of cowering fear as they cringed at the sharp Vietnamese commands.

About ten o'clock, a guard came in, followed by two others who came over to Reider and removed the yoke. His arms felt buoyant to him, crookedly accustomed to the yoke. The guards said nothing. Reider tried to flex his arms and stir the circulation of blood into his shoulders.

"I don't like this," said McGann. "I don't like this at all. I think you're in for trouble, Reider. I think that sadistic major of yours has got you marked."

They ate again at midday, the three of them still trying to get food into Sutherland, and when nothing happened that afternoon or evening, Reider began to feel relieved. That night, the silent Montagnard died.

Reider was kicked into consciousness at dawn by two guards. Major Lim was standing across the compound, holding open the gate. A third VC guard held the other side of the gate open, but Reider could not see what was going on outside. Lim signaled to one of the other guards to hold his side of the gate open and strode across the compound to Reider, stared at him, and smiled.

Reider inclined his head and said, "To what do we owe this unwelcome visit, Major?"

"I have a pleasant surprise for you, Sergeant. I have decided what should be done with you. It took me days to think what I should do because you prefer to act improperly. But I am not discouraged. I still believe you can be reeducated." He paused. Reider said nothing. "No clever comments? Don't tell me you have given up already. I didn't realize you were so willing to accept your role as a prisoner."

"I haven't quit," said Reider. "I'm just biding my time."

"Good, Sergeant. Very good. I would find no challenge with a pet so easily broken."

McGann and Meder rose and stood beside Reider. Lim was smiling as though he relished a private joke.

"Aren't you curious, Sergeant?" Lim asked. "Very well, I won't keep you waiting in suspense any longer."

He turned and barked in sharp Vietnamese. Slowly, from outside the gate, three guards pushed and pulled and shoved something inside the compound. Reider stared at Lim with all the contempt he could muster.

McGann put his arm on Reider's and said, "Don't do anything foolish. For God's sake, Reider, get hold of your senses."

"Let him go, Captain," said Lim. "The sooner I start his conditioning, the sooner he will be the well-trained pet I intend him to be."

The guards had brought in a bamboo cage. Two more guards entered with a ladder long enough to reach the beam that held the thatched roof. One held the ladder while one grasped the end of a rope attached to the bamboo cage, climbed up, and draped the rope over the beam. Pulling the cage four feet off the ground, the guard tied the rope to the beam.

Two of the VC guards grabbed Reider and tried to drag him to the cage, but he shook them off and walked under his own power, slid open the door of bamboo, and crawled inside. He crouched there; he had to, because of the smallness of the cage. He stared across the compound at the smiling Major Lim and McGann and Meder.

One of the guards left and returned with a bowl which he gave to Lim. "You will find, Sergeant," said Lim, coming over to the cage, "that eating the food we give our dogs will not supply you with much nourishment, but then it's up to you. The guards have been instructed to permit you to eat with the others as soon as you decide to eat in the way a dog eats."

Reider sat motionless in the cage, his arms around his knees, silent.

"We shall see, Sergeant," said Lim. "Hunger and thirst and time have strong effects on the will of any man—even you, Sergeant."

Lim took the bowl of food and threw it in Reider's face, then dropped the bowl in the dirt in front of the cage.

"We will see, Sergeant, when you decide in what

manner you want to live."

The guards brought soup and rice bowls in and placed them before McGann and Meder.

"The guards will remain," said Lim to McGann and Meder, "to supervise your feeding."

McGann spoke to Lim. "Let us help this man." He pointed to Sutherland who was lying against the wall, listlessly watching the proceedings. "He can't eat by himself, on all fours or any other way. Haven't you done enough to him?"

"By all means, gentlemen," said Lim. "By all means. Help your comrade. I will send in another ration for him. Just don't any of you interfere with my pet in the cage."

Lim turned and walked out.

Meder and McGann went over to Sutherland and lifted his head as gently as possible.

Sutherland groaned.

"Come on, Lieutenant, try to get some of this down," Meder coaxed.

They poured some of the soup down Sutherland's throat, and he gagged. The noise he made was reassuring; it indicated he was still alive and struggling. He even seemed to be improving, for he spoke. "More."

When they finished feeding Sutherland, McGann and Meder approached Reider's cage.

"Well, the writing's on the wall," said McGann. "You're really in for it, Reider."

Reider did not reply.

"We'll try to slip you some food at night," Meder said.

"No," said Reider. "I'm going to beat that little
upstart. He's never going to get me to crawl and
lick that slop up like a mindless pig." He grinned.
"Like the Japanese say, Shim-pai-nai."

"And what does that mean?" Meder asked.

"Don't sweat it." said Reider.

CHAPTER EIGHTEEN

Major Lim lit a Lucky Strike and drew the smoke deeply into his lungs. He had smoked his first Lucky in the Old Division area of Fort Bragg, North Carolina. Memories of the sand and pine-trees of the sprawling military reservation returned to him in a flood as Lim lounged in the doorway of his long house, leaning against the frame. He could see himself standing in the door of a classroom on Smoke Bomb Hill at the Special Warfare Center, taking a course on Psy War operations.

Lim chuckled sourly as he remembered the various techniques of counterinsurgency and area pacification that he had been taught. He had known they'd never work in Vietnam. They required men of integrity and honesty, both of which were very rare in the Saigon government. But the techniques might be useful when they took control of the country.

Lim shifted his position in the doorway, startling the starving dog that prowled in the debris at the corner of the house. The dog barked once and fled. At the other end of the village, Lim knew a handful of Chu Luk cadre were entertaining his men with tales of slaughter on their way to a rendezvous with a larger contingent at Ap Gu. He had worked with the Chu Luk before, and upon their arrival he had given them liberty to do as they pleased with any of his prisoners—save Reider. He had explained that he had special plans for that particular prisoner.

His thoughts returned to Fort Bragg. Lim had submitted numerous mock Combat Reports during his training, and each time he had scarcely concealed his smirk. He had been commended for his thoroughness, for the many maps and sketches he had offered, whenever practicable, on the reverse side of his reports. He had often been called "gung ho."

Cooking smoke curled up from behind a screen of ferns and turned toward the southern edge of the village. After he'd killed the American in Saigon, Lim had been a special instructor of guer-

illa warfare at a school south of Hanoi operated by
Vo Nguyen-Giap's Defense Ministry.

Laughter erupted and he coughed cigarette
smoke as he recalled his own U. S. Special
Forces instructors referring to the "thickly in-
fested" jungles of Southeast Asia and the "red
rebels," calling Vietnam "the enemy's kind of
country." He had done his personal best to make it
so.

A vague uneasiness slowly overcame Lim. He
straightened himself and stubbed the cigarette out
against the doorframe.

It was an old and recurring fear that had returned to haunt him, a spook that glimmered per-
iodically at the periphery of his inner vision. He
had yet to identify it precisely. What was it? The
fear, perhaps, that ultimate victory would go to
the Americans? That the much hated Caucasians
would find a way to burn back the forces Ho Chi
Minh believed unbeatable? But such thoughts
were counterrevolutionary, Lim concluded, too
swiftly to suit himself. If the NLF were ultimately
to be defeated, then Lim would have made all the
wrong moves. It would mean that he should have
chosen the path of Cao Ky and Thieu. But he felt
that he had to remain rooted in the belief that
destiny would deliver Vietnam into the hands of
the NLF. He could not forsake his faith. It was not
that he was particularly religious; but he was determined to remain adamantly idealistic—in the
Marxian sense.

He tried to summon up various maxims of

Chairman Mao he had memorized to dispel the vague fear that haunted him, but could not. What good were platitudes and profundities in the face of present danger? Poetry could not deflect bullets, nor deter the deadly mortar round. Material wealth could very well spell the eventual outcome of the war. Personnel could not be the deciding factor, no matter what numbers were hurled into the holocaust, because victory always came down to sheer firepower. Morale, however, was another matter. The scales of conflict could be decisively tilted should the psychological strength of one side or the other suddenly disintegrate. But he was dealing with the overall situation too realistically, not idealistically. What would logistics have to do with ultimate victory if the eventual outcome were written in the stars or in the cells of humanity aeons ago? Lim shuddered, grated his teeth, and cursed himself for allowing fear to overpower his thoughts. He must have been exposed to something in the United States that had somehow contaminated his confidence—infected his psyche with seeds of doubt.

He could feel the phantom pain in the non-existent part of his amputated arm.

Nothing in his life had remained stable, all things had changed—until he aligned himself with the philsophies of Mao and Lenin. Liberation from the Europeans. Ah! But perversely, Lim felt a twinge of guilt. He had absorbed the French culture, language, and sense of art, a mixture that did not reconcile well with communist doctrine. Ah, communist doctrine could be so Puritan. There was nothing Puritan about the French. But even Father Ho had said they would take and use much that the French had taught them. . . . Enough of this daydreaming! Back to business and good Sergeant Reider.

Reider. Beast. Moi!

Looking down, he saw the butt of the Lucky Strike he had smoked. He put his boot upon it and crushed the white paper and brown tobacco into oblivion.

CHAPTER NINETEEN

It was hot. Two days in the cage and Reider had begun to itch insufferably; he knew it would not be long until he had lice. His teeth felt as though they had been loosened, and numerous salt sores had developed on his body. Perspiration raced from his pores, and a glutinous swelling underneath his arms added to his discomfort. Incessant pricklings of the skin annoyed him most, and he was beginning to feel he had lost his hearing. He was weak now from lack of sustenance, and his tongue had swollen from lack of water. The daily sessions with Lim, as the Major strove to make him eat like a dog, had developed into an unceasing needlework on his nerves.

He longed to straighten his legs, to crawl from that bamboo straightjacket and walk, if just for a few feet, and he looked with nostalgia on the forced march from the field hospital to the compound. The memory of walking, of merely being able to walk, place one foot before the other, his eyes on objects other than bamboo bars. . . .

The smell of the decaying villager who had died on the cross permeated the compound. The heavy, sweetish stench made him want to gag. But in a way it was an aid to him. With that odor of decay at the back of his throat, he could not think of food. It was water he thought of most. How easily he had taken a drink back at the base, how he could pick up a tin cup, and the cup would be cold to the touch, and the water would be cool and clear in the container, and he conjured the look and taste on his tongue and palate. If he had a cup of that water that instant, he thought, he would slowly lower his tongue into it and take one miniscule droplet of water and roll it around inside his mouth as if it were a cool, translucent jewel. But he knew that he could not really stop with one small drop—he would gulp and gulp, until his stomach felt bloated with the precious liquid, and his tongue would be immersed and his mouth would not feel pinched and dry. The dream of water drove away the awful smell of the decaying man.

During this time in the cage, he began to summon up memories from his past, experiences he had had as a boy, because it was too much of an ordeal to sit there in that cage and look upon the compound and see McGann and Meder and Sutherland, who was better now, moving from one side to the other, while he sat in the cage, unable to talk to them, except under cover of night, unable to do anything but watch. It became easier for him to live inside his mind.

He was drowsing late one afternoon, hardly aware of his surroundings, when Lim strutted in, seized a short bamboo pole, and raked it back and forth across the bars.

"Wake up, Sergeant," said Lim. "Wake up at once."

Reider moved on the floor of the cage, grabbed the bars and looked out at Lim.

"Good afternoon, Sergeant. I see you are well. As I sat in my comfortable office, I was thinking of you. You know, do you not, that I think of you quite often? I was sitting there thinking that by now your legs must feel very tired and you would like to get out and walk around. Isn't that the way you feel, Sergeant?"

Reider did not reply. He stared at Lim.

"Sergeant, I am going to give you a nice surprise. At first I thought I would not do for you ever again, until you submitted. But you see, I have imagination. I can sit at my desk in there and know how you must feel, how you must want to stretch your legs. And so I have come out here to give you the opportunity to do so."

Still Reider did not respond.

"This traitorous villager, the one my predecessor placed on the cross, is beginning to be an irritant to me, Sergeant. The lesson has been given this village. It is no longer necessary for the man to remain hung so, upside down and rotting. And this will be your opportunity to exercise, Sergeant. I am going to let you out of the cage, and you are going to help our two friends bury the body. Sutherland is not yet strong enough. If you do this, you will be fed, and you will be given water."

Reider spoke. "Can we also bury the Montagnard?"

"No. It would be unkind to deprive you of his company just yet. You seem to have such affection for those savages."

Lim unlocked the door to the cage and pushed it up.

"Come out, Sergeant," said Lim.

Reider grabbed the bars with both hands and slowly swung his feet toward the ground. The cage was just high enough that he could not quite touch. He jumped the six inches or so to the ground, and his legs collapsed underneath him. He thought he had broken an ankle—the pain was intense—but he managed to get to his knees and crawl a few feet to the wall of the stockade, where he pulled himself upright, and stood shaking as he held onto the wall, watching Lim.

"Good, Sergeant," said Lim. "Good. I am glad to see that you have such spirit. Come."

Lim took Reider by the arm and half-carried him across the stockade toward McGann and Meder.

The three prisoners then moved to the cross and began to lower it. Lim directed this operation coolly, but Reider's hand brushed against the rotting flesh, and a large chunk came off and fell to the dirt. He gagged. McGann and Meder looked at him, their expressions evidence of their nausea. Lim then marched the three of them with the cross and three guards out the gate and into the jungle east of the village. They went about two hundred yards, Reider stumbling and falling because his legs were weak. They reached a small clearing. There Lim ordered them to put down the cross, and they did so.

"Now, Sergeant," said Lim. "You are going to earn your food and water for tonight. I want you to dig the grave."

"How?" Reider asked him.

"Come, Sergeant," said Lim. "Surely you must know how to dig a grave. Every dog knows how to bury a bone. And here you have a larger number of bones. You will get down on your hands and knees and you will dig the grave as a dog digs in the dirt, and when you have it big enough, we will lay our traitorous friend in it."

"No," said Reider.

"You will dig," said Lim. "And so will your friends."

"No."

Lim pulled his service revolver from his holster and aimed it at McGann and Meder. "Dig," he said again.

The two of them knelt on the ground and began picking at the earth with their hands.

"Dig, Sergeant," said Lim, pointing the pistol at him. "Dig."

"No."

"Do you want to die?" Lim shrieked. "Do you want to die so easily right here? Do you want me to shoot you here and let your two friends dig a grave twice as large so you may lie in it alongside this traitor?"

"You won't kill me," said Reider.

"I will kill you," said Lim. "I will kill you now."

"No, you won't," said Reider.

Lim's face was livid with rage. "Dig!" he screamed. "Dig, you animal, dig! You will be a dog, Sergeant. You will scratch and claw the earth with your paws!"

"Sat Cong, Moi!" said Reider.

Infuriated, Lim screamed at the top of his lungs. "You will not call me an animal, Sergeant! Ever again. You will not call me an animal. You are the animal. You are a dog. Dig."

"No," said Reider.

Lim's hand gripped the pistol butt so tightly his knuckles were bone white. His finger on the trigger, he placed the pistol barrel within an inch of Reider's chest. Lim's face was contorted with anger, and he stared directly into Reider's unyielding eyes. Lim's tongue flickered along his lips. "Dog," he hissed. "Dig. Dig, see the gun, Sergeant? Dig or I will shoot you."

"You won't kill me," said Reider. "And I won't dig. And if I die you will have lost. I will have won, Lim. Not you—me."

For a moment it seemed as if Lim would pull the trigger. His anger seemed uncontrollable. But he did not. He stepped back and pointed the pistol at McGann and Meder. "Dig the grave," he told them. "Dig it."

And as they dug, Lim kept the pistol pointed at Reider, waving it back and forth, lining the sights up on various parts of Reider's anatomy. Lim began to smile.

After the grave had been dug, and the cross and the dead villager placed within it, the dirt and mud pitched in upon the corpse, Lim marched the three of them back into the stockade and locked Reider back in the cage and left the stockade.

That night the guards who usually patrolled and checked to make sure that no food was given to Reider were not on duty. And McGann and Meder managed to take water to Reider as well as rice. Reider choked down the handfuls of rice and tipped his mouth through the bars of his cage to drink the water. McGann and Meder talked of escape, and of finding a way to get word outside. But the usual defeatism soon silenced them. Reider, however, lay awake long into the night devising strategems. Thoughts of freedom at last gave way to sleep.

The next morning, Lim was back in front of the cage again, raking his stick back and forth across the bars. Reider stared at him. Lim stopped and

ordered two guards to bring him a chair and place
it directly before the door of the cage.

"Sergeant, I have decided to talk to you," he
began. "You interest me. I want to know why you
keep fighting me. You will never escape from here.
The only escape there will ever be for you is death.
I could have killed you yesterday, by the grave, but
it was too easy. Why do you think I won't kill you?
I don't ask too much of you, Sergeant. I could tor-
ture you. I could burn you. I could put bamboo
slivers underneath your fingernails and light
them, or stake you out over some young bamboo
and let the shoots go through. But you are willing
to die, and I want to know why, Sergeant."

Reider stared at Lim through the bars of the
cage.

"Tell me, Sergeant, what was it like where you
came from? What part of the United States did
you come from? Was it the Midwest? Was it what
you call the South? What are you, Sergeant? I
want to know what makes you what you are. Come
now, Sergeant, don't be shy. Tell me. We will have
a good conversation. Where are you from?"

"Colorado."

"And where did you go to school? In Colorado?
You know I was in your country twice. But I never
went to Colorado. I was in North Carolina. And
California. It was hot in North Carolina. What is it
like in Colorado?"

"You don't give a damn what it's like there, Lim,
you're just playing games."

Lim ignored Reider's response. "So you grew up

in Colorado and you were drafted into the army, like so many of the young men in your country. And now, you are in a cage in a country you know nothing about. In a country you care nothing about, surrounded with a language you do not really speak and a culture you cannot comprehend. What is it that brought you here?"

"I'm a soldier," said Reider.

"That was the answer I thought you might give me," said Lim. "But, Sergeant, I am also a soldier. We are both professionals. There is no point in playing silly games. You are going to do what I want you to do. I am going to break you until you feel that you belong to me. You will be my dog. I will break you."

"No," said Reider. "You will not."

"Always a big talker, Sergeant. I do not think I shall let you talk around me. I think I will teach you to bark instead."

"You haven't taught me to crawl yet," said Reider.

"I will," said Lim. "When you become hungry enough and thirsty enough, you will crawl, and then bark, sit up, do tricks and follow me around on a rope, and I will show this entire village that the Americans are nothing but dogs for a North Vietnamese officer."

Reider's lips moved slightly.

"Are you trying to say something, Sergeant?"

Reider spat at him, and missed. The spittle lay in the dirt, a small, white globe that reflected the sun.

"Dogs do not spit at their masters," said Lim. He stood and left the stockade.

Three hours later he returned with guards, opened the cage, had the guards pull Reider out, and strapped a leather muzzle onto his face. Then Reider was shoved back into the cage, locked in again, and Lim departed with the guards.

CHAPTER TWENTY

That night Meder and McGann crawled over underneath the cage and spoke with Reider in whispers so the guards would not hear. It was an arduous task for Reider to speak because of the muzzle, even though his hands were free to pull it a little away from his mouth. There was no way he could get it off.

"Can you breath okay in that thing, Sarge?" Meder asked him.

"I'm okay, I guess," said Reider. "Where's Sutherland?"

"He's still very weak. I hope he pulls out of this," McGann said.

"Listen. You said that the choppers came over every once in a while. Right?"

"They used to," said McGann. "They used to come every two or three days, but I haven't seen any since you've been here."

"All right. They'll be back," said Reider. "We've got to be ready to signal them somehow. It's the only way we're ever going to get out."

"I don't know how," Meder said. "We've been through this thing a hundred times, and we just haven't come up with a way to do it."

The following day, Lim ordered the crumpled, disintegrating body of the Yard to be removed. McGann and Meder and Reider followed Lim out of the stockade, carrying the reeking corpse slung between them. They struggled along over the same ground to the same clearing, stumbling and plodding, their lungs clogged with the stench.

Lim seemed in a most jovial mood. Reider puzzled over what new tricks Lim might be planning. Would he try to force him to dig with his hands again? Lim did not. When they reached the clearing, there were three shovels thrust upright in the earth, and he and McGann and Meder dug the grave. When they were finished, Lim kicked the body of the Yard into the hole and ordered them to fill it with the loose, damp earth. When they were through with their task, they stuck the shovels back in the dirt and Lim marched them back toward the stockade.

Shortly before they arrived at the gate, Reider heard something. He stopped—ears straining for the sound. It was the distant beating of chopper blades. McGann nudged Reider. "Don't get your hopes up, Sarge," he muttered. "Most of the time they just pass right over the village. Once in a while they come over at night and cut their spots on, but you know how hard it is to see anything from up there. We've been praying for 'em to come in and find something for months—they never do. This camouflage netting keeps us from being seen at all."

Lim sauntered over. "Your American helicopters do not see you here, and they never will. Do not be foolish enough to try to signal them. If you *were* able to bring them in, you would all be killed before they could get to you."

As Lim locked Reider in his cage with a burst of crude laughter, Reider put his mind to the problem. By nightfall, he thought he had an idea. The cage was tied by a rope to one of the beams, and at the end of the beam, on the outside of the building was one of the attaching claws for the camouflage netting. If he could swing the cage hard enough, pump it up like a swing, then maybe the beam would start to jerk, and the netting would move, and perhaps the movement would be observed by the choppers.

"What do you think, McGann?" Reider asked that night.

"Christ, Sergeant, I don't know. I really don't. If we try to signal those choppers and we goof it, that

Major's gonna castrate us for sure. But if we could signal them, maybe they'd drop down and chop up enough of these VC so we could make a break over the wall. If we could get out in the open, where they could see us, they could get a Mike Force to us before the Cong got us again. It might be worth a chance. What about you, Meder?"

"I don't know," said Meder. "It sounds pretty risky to me. You really think you can move that beam enough to have the movement spotted from the chopper?"

"Maybe," said Reider. "It's worth a try. You say they come over every couple or three days?"

"They did before you got here."

"You guys ever try to time it? Is there any patrol pattern?"

"Not that I can tell," said McGann. "Once in a while they'll come over at night, but usually it's in the daytime. Most of the time they just hover over the village, check it out, sniff around overhead. But they never get close enough to detect anything."

"Well, next time the choppers come over, I'm gonna try it. I want you guys to help me. As soon as we hear them, you come over to the cage and start swinging it, and I'll pump it up. There must be a couple of hundred pounds on that rope. It ought to be enough to jerk that beam around some."

"Okay," said Meder. "We'll give it a try. But it sure as hell better work."

Reider awoke early next morning. He was stiff again, and he was beginning to feel as though he

would lose the use of his arms and legs. He had not
had a chance to wash since the field hospital. His
gums were exceedingly tender and beginning to
swell, and his teeth had a film over them, despite
his efforts to clean them with his fingers. He was
also making daily discoveries of itches and afflic-
tions of the skin, especially underneath his arms.
The sweat had collected and dried there until the
hair was stiff and stinking. And his groin had in-
numerable itches where the sweat had plastered
his legs. When he scratched his scalp, hair came a-
way with large flakes of dead skin, grease and dirt.
His beard was growing long and thick—and filthy.

At ten o'clock that morning, two VC guards
came to the cage. Lim was not with them. One unlocked the cage, and the other levelled a rifle at
Reider's head. He grabbed hold of the bars and
slowly let himself down, trying not to fall. But he
could not control himself and landed on his hands
and knees in front of one of the guards. While the
one guard held the rifle, the second guard
screamed at him and started to jerk at his clothing. Reider could not understand what he wanted,
but then the VC made gestures that did not re-
quire translation and Reider complied and stripped. The VC with the rifle stepped back a few
paces and the other guard took the dirty bundle of
clothing. Then they took his muzzle off, motioned
Reider back into the cage and locked it.

Meder came across to the cage. "What the hell
was that all about?" he asked.

"I don't know," said Reider. "But I have a hunch

old Lim is starting in on me for sure now. I don't
know if I was glad to get rid of those clothes or
not. They were sure beginning to stink, but I've got
a hunch I'm going to miss them."

Late in the afternoon two guards came back
carrying food and water for McGann, Meder, and
Sutherland—and nothing for Reider. They stood
by the compound gate watching the prisoners to
see that no one slipped any food to Reider. One
guard, a particularly fat youth they had nicknamed Goo Face, was watching Reider all the time
the others ate—just watching. McGann was
picking at his food without eating, and Reider
knew that he felt guilty for not being able to slip
any across, but Reider also knew that McGann
was as hungry as he. They were all on short
rations, and he did not blame the man for wanting
to wolf his food, even if it meant Reider would
have to watch the food consumed.

When the others had eaten, the guards picked
up the bowls and turned on their heels and left.

McGann crawled across the compound and sat
by the cage.

"Reider," he said, "I think that son of a bitch is
going to try and starve you to death."

"He can try," Reider replied.

"But what the hell are we going to do?" asked
McGann. "If they have old Goo Face and that other
punk in here every time we get chow, we aren't
ever going to be able to slip you any. Goo Face was
watching you and the other one was watching us,
and if we had tried to slip any rice into our jackets
they'd have tried to kill us."

"That's what they were here for," said Reider.

"Well, look, Sergeant, you can't last more than a week or so without eating. Hell, we can sneak water to you. They can't watch the water jug all the time. But, Jesus, you can't go too long without eating."

"I know," said Reider. "I'm just hoping those choppers come back around. I don't know about the rest of you guys, but I don't feel much like sitting here for the next four or five years, and I sure as hell don't like the idea of starving to death."

There was no food for Reider for the next day. Goo Face and the other guard, whom McGann had nicknamed Archie, stood inside the compound all during the feeding and watched with gimlet-eyed scrutiny. There would be no chance of their sneaking any food to Reider.

He tried not to think about food, but that became extra difficult by the end of the following day. He did not sleep well at night and he began to dream of meals he'd eaten. In one dream he ate a whole bowl of chocolate ice cream, and he had never even liked chocolate ice cream. He began to feel weaker.

On the morning of the third day he slept until nearly noon. When he awoke, his head felt light. McGann came over and gave him some water, but Reider was getting very tired of water; it was having a strange effect on him. It would fill his stomach, but it gave him no satisfaction, and he began to hate it because it could not assuage his hunger.

At noon on the third day, Goo Face and Archie

came in with the bowls of food. They forced Meder
and McGann to feed Sutherland first; then they
marched them across and sat them down in front
of the cage and forced them to eat in front of
Reider. McGann and Meder tried to eat slowly at
first, glancing up into Reider's face. Reider would
have given a lot to have looked into his own face at
that moment. McGann and Meder tried to look
away, but each time either one of them did, Goo
Face would scream and jerk his rifle up. Finally, Mc-
Gann could take no more and he gulped his food
down as hurriedly as he could swallow it.

"Don't worry about it, McGann," said Reider.
"Just get it over with as quickly as you can. It's a
little tough to watch."

When McGann and Meder had finished, Goo
Face and Archie took the bowls away again, and
that night Reider could not sleep at all.

After that day, each twenty-four hours seemed
to blur into a kind of nothingness, with noon the
glaring punctuation point of horror when he was
forced to watch McGann and Meder eating. Even
when he turned his eyes away, he cold hear them
eating, and he could almost taste the food. Worse
yet, he could imagine what it was like to be eating.
Those rotten pieces of fish and the handfuls of rice
became delicacies in his mind.

Reider began to sleep most of the day as well as
most of the night. When McGann came over and
talked to him, he had to concentrate very hard,
because the words sometimes became indistinct.
And it was so hard for him to concentrate. He tried

to think of escape, but his mind seemed to wander a great deal. He would sometimes spend half an hour trying to regain a thought. And after what was perhaps a week, he did not think much at all—he just leaned back against the bamboo bars, and dreamed, sometimes of home, sometimes of Japan, sometimes of the Montagnards, and the mountains, and boot camp. Sometimes he wondered if he were going mad. He could no longer stomach a cup of water. But he did not think of food any more—it seemed somehow obscene. And even when he watched McGann and Meder eating, he did not want any of it. He began to think of himself as being pure—superior—because he did not have to eat. But sometimes, later in the day, he was sure that such thoughts meant his mind was going.

One day—Reider was no longer sure how many days it had been—Goo Face and Archie were followed in by Lim, who watched the feeding, and looked at Reider. Reider held the bars of the cage and stared back. He could tell by looking at his hand that he was starting to lose his strength. His wrists were very thin, and the skin on his hands was wrinkled, almost like an old man's. His knuckles were bony. He tried to squeeze down hard on the bamboo bar, but he found that it was all he could do to keep his fingers wrapped around it. His arm was a string of tendons wrapped around with loose, sagging skin. It came to him that he could not last much longer.

When McGann and Meder had finished and

Sutherland had been fed, Goo Face and Archie took the bowls away and Lim came walking toward the cage.

"Good afternoon, Sergeant," Lim greeted him.

Reider did not reply. He squatted there and rocked a little bit and looked at Lim.

"Sergeant, you don't seem to be eating very well."

Reider stared at him.

Lim walked around the cage twice, observing Reider as though he were a specimen in a zoo. Lim seemed to think him so unusual, Reider half expected the major to produce a camera and take pictures of him.

Reider stared straight ahead as Lim walked round and round, not following him with his eyes. Lim stopped after the third circuit, and came very close to the cage and looked Reider in the eyes.

"Sergeant, if you do not get something to eat soon, you are going to die," said Lim. "Do you know that?"

"Yes," said Reider.

"Then, Sergeant, you must know that I don't want you to die. I told you back in the jungle, when we were first together, that I didn't want you to die until I was ready for you to die. So I am going to give you a chance, Sergeant."

Lim turned on his heel and went to the gate, opened it and waved outside. Goo Face came back carrying a large bowl of stew, not rice, not fish, not thin, dried strips of anything, but a hot stew. Reider could smell it all the way across the stockade. It was beef stew, and it had potatoes in it and carrots, and a thick gravy, and Reider was afraid of what was coming, afraid of what he would do, and afraid to smell that marvelous aroma, and thinking of what it would taste like in his mouth—the soup, the carrot, the soft potato, the tender strips of beef—Reider's hands began to shake.

Lim had Goo Face bring the bowl over and set it down in front of the cage, and then he brought in another small bowl of water.

"Let him out," Lim ordered.

Goo Face opened the door of the cage, grabbed Reider by the hands and pulled him out. He fell forward in the dirt, his face pressed to the earth, his knees shaking. He could not even sit up. He managed to get up on his elbows, his knees still shaking, and he looked up. Lim was standing above him.

"Well, Sergeant," said Lim, "you seem to be very much the way I want you this time. You even look like a dog, Sergeant. A skinny, starving one. I think I like you the way you look right now, down there on the dirt. Nothing distinguishes you from a dog now, Sergeant. You are unable to get on your feet and walk like a man. You have no clothes on to prove you are civilized. You are a starved mongrel looking for a handout. And I have some scraps for you here, and I want you to eat, Sergeant. I want you to crawl along the ground to the bowl, and I want you to stick your face in the bowl and eat. And when you are through eating, you are going to stick your face in the water and

you are going to drink it, and then maybe I will
take you out of the cage."

Reider could not stand the feeling in his stom-
ache. His gut was turning around and over and
fluttering almost as if he were having a convul-
sion. His mouth would not stop watering and the
saliva drooled and dripped from his chin and fell
in the dirt in front of him. He tried to keep himself
together. He almost felt as if he could cry. He wanted that bowl of stew very badly. But somehow
from somewhere in the back of his mind—and
even he at that time was not sure where—came
some strength, a very small seed of strength, and
he managed to raise his eyes all the way to Lim's
face and say, "No."

Lim stood there staring at him for a full minute.
Then he kicked at Reider, and Reider did not have
enough energy to move out of the way, and Lim's
boot caught him by the ear and bright flashes of
pain exploded in his head. He fell over and lay on
the ground. Lim was furious, screaming at Goo
Face as he jumped up and down in a frenzy.
Finally he calmed down a little and pulled his service pistol from its holster. Kneeling down, he put
the barrel to Reider's head.

"Sergeant, I am going to give you ten seconds to
move toward that bowl, and if you do not, I am going to kill you right now."

"Won't," Reider rasped. "Won't! You won't kill
me. It's too easy." And Reider fell asleep, lying
there in the dirt with Lim screaming at him.

When Reider woke up the next day he was back

in the cage. McGann and Meder were eating and
Goo Face and Archie were watching them, just as
they had been each day since he could remember.
And when Goo Face and Archie had taken the
bowls away, Lim came back in, and Goo Face and
Archie went over to Sutherland and picked him up
and dragged him across the compound and threw
him in front of the cage. The guards withdrew and
then returned with the bowl of stew. Reider did
not think he could stand it this time. The guards
opened the cage and he stumbled out again, lying
in the dirt, smelling the stew, and looking at Sutherland, whose half-closed eyes showed that he was
semi-conscious.

"Sergeant," said Lim, "you are going to crawl
over to the bowl and eat, as I told you to do yesterday. If you do not, I am going to take out my pistol
and shoot Sutherland."

Reider couldn't let Sutherland die for him, even
though privately he was convinced that Sutherland was going to die anyway. He managed to
raise his eyes and look at Lim, and he thought
maybe he could try and bluff him through. He
tried to ignore the smell of the food and the heat
and the dirt and the sour, glutinous feel of his
body, and looked at Lim and said, "No."

Lim jerked his pistol out, knelt beside Sutherland and placed the muzzle of the weapon against
Sutherland's temple.

"Move, Sergeant," Lim ordered. "Now."

Reider glared at him, hating him, trying to pour
his fury from his eyes, all the hatred he had left in

him. And then he crawled on his knees and elbows over to the bowl of stew and put his face down in it, and started to eat. And when his face got close to the bowl he could not resist the smell any more, and he shoved his mouth into the warm stew and began eating, gobbling, his forearms holding the bowl tightly. He choked several times on the chunks of beef, and the food was on the dirt and on his face and on his arms and in his nose and he did not care, because it was food, and he almost felt like crying with joy because it was so good. But he could not eat as much as he wanted; his stomach felt strange. Yet a feeling of warmth was coming back into his body, a feeling of strength. More will power than he had felt in weeks. He went over to the water bowl and before Lim could stop him, he picked it up with his hands and drank. Lim screamed at him and dashed the bowl from his hands.

"You are not sincere, Sergeant," he said. "You are not sincere. You do not mean it. You did that just to gain the strength to fight me. Well, I will show you, Sergeant, where your sincerity has brought you."

Lim put his pistol to the back of Sutherland's head and squeezed the trigger. The Russian 7.62 bullet smashed its way into Sutherland's brain, blowing bone, brains and gore all over the dirt and the spilled stew.

CHAPTER TWENTY-ONE

Furiously, Reider sprang at Lim, but the butt of Lim's pistol struck the base of his skull and Reider fell.

When he regained consciousness, Reider found himself back in the cage. Sutherland's body had been removed. McGann sat near the bars staring at him.

"You awake, Reider?" he asked with incredulity.

"If you're not a dream, I am."

"Listen, Reider, that bastard's gonna kill all of us. I know you don't want to knuckle under to him, but me and Meder have been talking about it, and I don't see any need of us getting zapped just because you and Lim got this personal thing going. I mean, I know it's pretty rotten, and you don't like what he's doing, but that's making it even worse for us. I think we better try what you said the next time the choppers come around."

"Okay," Reider mumbled. "Look, McGann, I'm sorry as hell about Sutherland. I didn't think he would do it. I mean, that's why I crawled to the food. I didn't think he would do it."

"There's a lotta fight in you, Reider," said McGann. "And a hell of a lot of what we used to call downright cussedness, too. I don't think Lim's quite figured that out yet. But it makes things damn dangerous for me and Meder. I figure you better play along with him tomorrow if he comes in for chow time. Just go ahead and eat, even if you have to crawl. Keep it up, and maybe the choppers will come back and we can get out of here. Okay?"

"Okay," Reider agreed. "I will."

The next few days were a nightmare. Reider crawled and ate his food, lying in the dirt, hating each mouthful as he prostrated himself, loathing Lim, who taunted Reider, and laughed, and even brought village children to watch the American groveling, eating like a dog. And when Reider had eaten that way for a week, Lim brought in a large dog on a leash, ordered Reider out of the cage and

forced him to lie in the dirt beside the dog. Then
Reider and the dog were fed together. And again
Lim brought the villagers, and they all stared at
Reider. But Reider's strength was returning. He
could feel it in his hands and arms, in the way his
wrists fleshed out again and the way the tendons
of his arms became flexible. Reider began to look
forward to his crawling. It stretched his muscles.
He silently mapped strategies for escape. He was
beginning to feel much better, as Lim kept the
stew flowing steadily. McGann and Meder fed on
rice and fish. And Reider felt confident that when
the choppers came over again he would be strong
enough to flee the compound—and he would have
his revenge: Lim would die.

Lim left Reider alone for a full week, but late in
the afternoon, on what Reider thought was a Saturday, although he had no reason to think so, that
changed. Goo Face and Archie came in and stationed themselves before the cage. Then, while Goo
Face held a rifle on him, Archie went out the gate
and returned with a leather leash and collar.
Reider resolved to refuse. But then he reconsid-
ered. It was a way out of the stockade, he reason-
ed. With the strength he had gathered, he might be
able to give Archie a paralyzing kick, nail Goo
Face, and escape into the jungle. He could return
for Lim later. So he waited while Archie slipped
the leash on him and motioned impatiently for
Reider to move. He did, crawling out the gate and
thirty yards beyond to the command hut where
Lim stood in the doorway.

When Reider reached the foot of the steps that led up the porch of the hut, he saw that Lim had been drinking heavily. Lim held a bottle of bourbon in his hand. His eyes were reddened. Lim leaned against the doorframe and gave a slurred order in Viet. Archie handed Lim the end of the leash in front of the door, and Lim gazed down at Reider. Reider was led into the command hut and left to stand before a large couch which sat against the far wall; a desk was behind him. Seated on the couch was a young and attractive Vietnamese girl who stared at the naked Reider curiously, her eyes going wide for a moment and then narrowing slightly as her gaze returned to Lim. A quart of Scotch stood on the table and Lim swapped the bottle of bourbon for the Scotch, poured himself a drink, cleared his throat, and smiled at Reider.

"Today, Sergeant," Lim assured him, "you are going to perform for me. My one pet will do his tricks for my other pet. My dog will perform for my kitten." He laughed.

The girl stared at Reider.

"Sit," Lim ordered him. "Sit."

Reider did not move.

"Sit, damn you!" Lim screamed as he yanked on the leash.

Reider choked.

"Dog," snarled Lim. "You will sit when I command."

Lim kicked Reider, and the leash flew from his hand. Quickly, Lim retrieved it and pulled Reider up onto his knees and elbows again.

"Send him out," the girl pleaded. "Please. Send him out."

Lim snarled at her, "My dog will perform for you."

"I do not wish to see it," she protested.

Lim slapped her viciously in the mouth, and she fell back heavily upon the couch. Lim pulled the leash, choking Reider, pulling hard against him.

With his breath shut off, Reider felt himself sinking toward a sitting position when he heard a faint but familiar sound. He hoped with all his heart it was not a product of his imagination. It was the distant buzz of rotary blades.

Lim jerked the leash and pulled Reider along the floor to the open door of the hut. There Lim listened, staring up through the camouflage netting and the trees of the jungle. In the distance, a squadron of choppers throbbed toward them, their course in a direct line with Lim's hut, the roar of their motors growing stronger, louder, closer with every second.

"Maybe one of the villagers ratted on you, Lim," Reider gasped.

"Shut up!"

"Shut up!" Lim screamed as he kicked Reider in the kidneys.

Reider fell to the floor, groaning. From where he lay on the hard wood looking up at the vertical rectangle of doorway, he saw the most beautiful sight he had ever seen in his life: five, then ten Cobra helicopters coming in at treetop level, each cam-

ouflaged fuselage a dull glow of purposeful
menace.

Lim dropped the leash and ran from the
command hut, yelling in Viet as his men dashed
for the hidden antiaircraft guns. Troops rushed
around the stockade to their duty stations as the
choppers came in lower and slowed over the trees.
The lead chopper passed over the village and
dropped toward the camouflage net. Lim shouted
for his men to open fire, and they obeyed as
tracers shrieked from the hovering choppers. Bed-
lam ensued.

Reider saw Goo Face and Archie running toward the hut. The moment was critical: he had no
more than half a minute and so swiftly he rose and
dived out the open rear window of the hut, tumb-
ling onto the ground outside.

CHAPTER TWENTY-TWO

Free! Reider fled into the jungle, away from the choppers and the firing and the screaming VC, but his strength was not so great as he had imagined and he tired in a few minutes, walked again until he could breathe more easily and then resumed his running.

He emerged from the trees into a sea of grass that rose to a level with his waist, broken only by an occasional stunted tree and rocky ground. It was getting dark, but he could see well enough to

avoid obstacles and make good time. A platoon of
Cong crossed ahead of him, over where the trees
began again, but he dove into the grass and the VC
passed without seeing him. He had only a vague
idea of which direction he was moving in, as it was
dusk, but he thought it was east, and as long as it
was away from the camp he was unmindful of his
route. He moved wearily, hunched low, sweating
heavily, with only his head peering nervously over
the dry tips of the waving grass, which rattled
with a dry and dreadful noise as he brushed
through. Reider's heart thrummed excitedly as he
told himself again and again that he had escaped.
Ecstatic with the fact that he had gotten out, he
rose and resumed his flight.

Around midnight, back in the jungle terrain
again, he stumbled into a village. The hut nearest
him loomed out of the dark suddenly, and he almost walked into its wall before he could stop. He
hit the dirt behind the hut and listened carefully.

The village was silent.

Crawling slowly, softly around the edge of the
hut to the doorway, he listened intently for a few
minutes. There was only the regular, even breathing of one occupant. Then he crawled carefully
into the hut and halted beside the man who lay
sleeping alongside one wall. He edged over next to
him, slipped the leash around his throat and
strangled him. Reider's victim kicked but once,
and then lay still. Fortunately, the villager was a
large man, approaching obesity by Asian stand-
ards, and unusually tall. Reider stripped the

clothing from the corpse, dressed himself, and then rummaged around inside the hut until he found a long machete protruding from the bamboo of the far wall. Reider took the machete and then crept from the hut, ears alert for pursuers, and ducked back into the jungle.

He struggled to recall all that he could of his survival training, as well as the savvy he had acquired from the Montagnards. He knew that the jungle could be an ally as well as an adversary. It could hide him, protect him, provide him with food and water, and it could kill him if he ran counter to its ways. The worst enemy was a snake —a little, short snake perhaps as thick as an index finger. He couldn't remember its name, but it was supposed to go for the eyes, and when it did, you were dead. Snakes. Scorpions. Spiders. Who gave a shit? He was free. He padded along doggedly, his tired eyes wary of every hanging creeper and bush that brushed across the trail he had taken from the village.

Soon he was surrounded with heavy dampness and chill among the trees. The trail curled in and out, around the trees and creepers, sank beneath the branches and clammy foliage. At what he guessed to be about three o'clock in the morning, he stopped and crawled a dozen feet from the path into the undergrowth, ripped a clear patch in the vegetation and lay down on the wet earth. He was in desperate need of sleep, but a scream in the night blanketed his skin with pimples of terror until he identified the cry to be that of a monkey.

Other night creatures' eerie screeches abruptly split the heavy silence, and as he tried to get comfortable, he heard rustlings in the underbrush. He soon became conscious of the odor exuding from his body, and his nostrils wrinkled in distaste. He hoped he could locate a moving stream of water soon and bathe. As for his thirst, Reider determined to lick the dew off leaves after daylight. Exhausted, he fell asleep.

At dawn, his eyes opened to the rose colored light that filtered through the emerald foliage above him. He clambered stiffly, heavy with fatigue, out of his nest and returned to the well-worn trail. It was heading south, he saw. Breakfast consisted of berries from a bush. They tasted sweet, like a mixture of fruits, and he rationalized that if they tasted all right they were safe for consumption. But the berries had an acidic tang, and although they helped assuage his hunger and thirst, still his appetite was far from sated.

Every thirty minutes he stopped to rest, breathing deeply, accusing himself of laggardness. He ate more berries and some flower buds, and moved ahead steadily until, late in the afternoon, the smell of a wood fire reached him. The pungent odor probably meant that there was a village near. He dropped to his hands and knees and crawled forward cautiously until he reached the edge of a clearing dotted with a dozen huts. Two or three natives in loincloths meandered through the area.

Reider retreated into the jungle to lie down and watch for a while. He hoped that this was not a VC controlled village—or at least not completely VC.

As he watched a native woman draw water from a wooden trough, he was surprised to feel stirrings of sexual excitement in himself. Near the trough lay a pile of edible roots, for the natives collected them, and deposited them near the fire for cooking. He lay watching them till nightfall, which came swiftly as usual. A heavy cloud cover hid the thousands of stars. He waited until deep into the night and crept into the village, standing furtively over the water trough to slake his thirst, lifting his head at each unfamiliar sound. The coals of the cooking fire shifted slightly on the opposite side of the clearing, but no one emerged from the huts. Reider helped himself to a handful of the edible roots, and then slipped back to the trail just beyond the village.

He walked for half a mile before he knelt and wormed his way into the underbrush again, and there he ate the vegetables he had stolen. He slept eight hours this time; it was after dawn of the next day before he awakened.

He knew now that the strength he had thought considerably improved in the prison camp was not all that much, and he decided to stay off the trail in the underbrush and steal from the village for a while until his strength had time to build.

He went further off the trail, cleared a patch of ground, and placed leaves and ferns upon the spot. He sank down upon his mat thankfully. It was comfortable, and there he fell asleep again. Around noon he rose and searched for berries and ate his fill. Near dusk he found an unwary monkey he killed with a well-thrown rock. Raw monkey meat was not as bad as he thought it would be; at least, it was meat. The next morning he felt better, and he decided to resume his trek again after all. The memories of Lim and the camp and the fear of being recaptured spurred him on.

That afternoon he came to a narrow road—dirt, but a road—winding through the jungle trees, just wide enough to thin the tangle overhead so a misty brightness came through. He crossed the road cautiously, but then a sound ahead of him reached his ears and he started running. There it was: a small trickle of water flowed slowly into a hollow. The water seemed to be seeping from the rocks and it was a little dirty, but Reider lapped it like a dog and sucked with his lips at the tiny rivulets that passed from crevices in the earth and among the rocks.

He made another nest for himself and stayed there for a night and a day, eating berries, resting, sleeping, and watching the road.

He saw several bicycles wheel down the road, and an occasional battered truck, and once a staff car of North Vietnamese regulars. The staff car convinced him he should leave the road in the morning.

That day his progress became more difficult. The trail was overgrown, and he had to hack his way through brambles and bushes with the machete. The undergrowth tore his skin, lashing and clutching at his legs. Before the day had

ended, he was deeply scratched and feared the
scratches might fester in the filth he could not
wash away. All that day he went without water,
and found little fruit, and the hunger that night
was nearly as agonizing as he had felt in the cage.
He decided the hunger was a result of his having
eaten regularly, even if only the berries. The thirst
was almost as severe as his hunger, for he had
found no water that day. He was slightly light-
headed, and his breath came quickly, in little
gasps. His tongue had swollen, and his mouth felt
leathery. He slept fitfully that night. The next day
he found practically no fruit save a few unripened
mangoes. The first was so bitter, he couldn't eat a
second. That night he slept little, moving as soon
as it was light enough to see, dizzy and driven by
the dream of water.

Around noon he came upon a small stream and
for a hour he lay looking dreamily at it. This time
he made another nest, and stayed for four days.
He became more cunning about food. He nibbled
small roots and young green bamboo shoots. The
taste was raw and earthy, with strains of bitter-
ness. Once he found a small green frog, which he
promptly killed, and succeeded in eating the pale
flesh raw. An hour after he vomited.

On the fourth day of his stay in the new nest he
got dysentery, and for hours he suffered as the
watery feces gushed in spurts, with new sets of
cramps squeezing and pushing his guts. He lay in
the soft, matted grass and felt as if he would have
been better off dead. The dysentery passed next

day, and Reider decided to walk. He needed another village where he could steal more food. He paced himself slowly that night, covering about six miles, because he was very shaky, and he found several small grass snakes whose firm white meat stopped the cramps and rumbling of his stomach. During the next day he slept, and at dusk he started walking again. It was cooler to travel at night.

Towards dawn the next day, the trail opened out into a clearing, and Reider ducked into the undergrowth, worked his way forward and stopped at the edge, where he studied the dark shadows of huts. As the dawn broke, he observed the settlement to be sizeable. There were more than forty flimsy huts. The natives became active at first light, and Reider fought with himself to stifle the scream he felt when he smelled the meat cooking over big fires. He bent forward to ease the pains in his stomach. But he was afraid to walk into the village. He had no way of knowing whether they were friend or foe.

He watched the village all that day, knowing that he was probably going to need help to reach Saigon, to get anywhere out of the jungle, and he had to admit to himself that he had no idea where he was going, other than generally southeast. The odds against his running across a Viet patrol were not good, but he did not relish the idea of a steady diet of berries and raw snake and monkey and not enough water. He was in better physical condition than he had been while confined to the cage, but it was merely a matter of time before he exhausted himself and collapsed.

After nightfall he crawled out of the underbrush, walked across the hard-packed earth, passing a couple of natives who failed to see him in the dark, and stopped at the door of a hut he had picked out earlier in the day. The man he had seen walking in and out of the hut had seemed unusual. Reider had tried to pinpoint precisely why the man appeared ill at ease. It was something about the way the man carried himself and the way in which he conversed with other villagers, as though he were a big-city boy. He did not have the look of a villager, or the mannerisms of a villager. Throughout the entire day Reider had seen no VC or any radio equipment, or anything to indicate that there were VC around, and so he had decided to take this chance.

He walked inside the door opening of the hut and stood for a few seconds, taking it all in: the mud floor, the bamboo table, the man sitting there. Then he asked the Vietnamese if there were any VC in the area. The man in the hut stared at him, face betraying no emotion. He replied in Vietnamese that there were no VC.

"I have no food," Reider told him.

"Where are you from?" the man asked him.

Reider pointed toward the northwest.

"Are there others?"

"No," Reider replied.

"Wait, then." And the man went out the door.

Shortly the man returned. Behind him was an old man with a thin face and a few white hairs on

his head, and Reider felt a flood of relief. The old
man wore a St. Christopher's medal, suspended
from a chain that hung almost to his navel.

Half an hour later he was lying comfortably on
the floor of the hut. He had consumed two jars of
water and eaten a piping hot curry that left him
gasping for breath, and he had swollen his mouth
out further with more water. He slept peacefully
that night. In the early morning, a young Vietnamese man who appeared to be about twenty,
awakened Reider and introduced himself as Xuan
San.

Xuan San had short-cropped black hair, a
rather thin face and tight lips. He was brisk, but
friendly, as he informed Reider that VC had passed through the village a few weeks earlier and
raped several of the young women. That was one
of the reasons why the man to whom Reider had
spoken had been friendly. Xuan San confirmed
the fact that the man in the hut was not a native of
the village. He was from the south. Xuan San was
very evasive about what the man did for a living or
what position he held, but he reassured Reider
that the head man was friendly, and therefore, the
village was, too. They chatted for awhile of other
things, and then suddenly Xuan San asked, "What
are you planning to do?"

Reider deliberated for a moment, and discov-
ered that he had not yet decided. He wanted to
avenge himself and kill Lim, but he wanted to rejoin his own forces first. They talked a while
longer, and then Xuan San left, suggesting that

Reider eat and rest.

And for two days Reider did little else but rest
and eat curried rice, sweet boiled roots, and green
shoots. One of the old head man's younger wives
brought him jars of water and he washed, and two
village women dressed the lacerations that were
beginning to fester, removed his filth-encrusted
clothing, boiled the garments for hours, and returned them to him, clean but stained with sweat
splotches. The odor had been boiled away.

On his third day in the village, Reider wandered
among the huts, meeting the villagers, sitting
quietly and watching the Vietnamese women
pound the grain to paste. Later that afternoon he
sat and talked with the head man about the VC
and the Vietnamese. The old man spoke freely,
voicing his concern for the village.

Reider asked the head man whether all of the
villagers were trustworthy. The head man smiled
and answered yes and reminded Reider that the
leader of the village was before him and that his
people obeyed his will. There were no VC there,
nor were there those in the village who sympa-
thized with the VC.

At dusk the following day, Reider walked to the
end of the village, where he stood before the burial
hut and stared at the wooden statue above it. The
figure held an amulet in its hands, and Reider
marveled at these people who waged war from
thatched huts and erected wooden statues to ward
off evil spirits. They wanted nothing more than to
be themselves and live their lives in peace and

have children who would grow to maturity in a
tiny village in the heart of the jungle. And he began
to feel his convictions strengthened as to why he
was in the war, and the fear of the cage and of Lim
vanished. He was eager to be in uniform once
more. He would take a few weeks' leave in Japan,
and then he would return to find his major. Lim
belonged to him now; to no other—not even to the
People's Army of Liberation. The day would come,
he firmly believed; he would find Lim, and he
would have his one hundred and thirty pounds of
flesh.

Around noon the next day Xuan San came to tell
Reider that he would guide him down the trail to a
village five miles distant. There were no VC there,
and Xuan San knew the head man. From there
Reider could get to the road and might even se-
cure transportation south and east to the American forces. Xuan San told Reider they would go
the next morning early. Reider fell asleep that
night, confident that within a week he would be
back in a bunk and in uniform with some real food
in him, feeling like a man and a soldier and something more than a harried animal, running scared
and alone. No dream could have been sweeter.

At dawn, Xuan San came and they said goodbye
to the head man. Most of the villagers had assembled, their silent gaze fixed upon him, the
women wearing rough shawls, a few with babes in
their arms. None waved goodbye, but they all
watched him leave. He hoped he would be able to
return one day and repay them for their kindness
and protection.

The village Xuan San took him to was much bigger than the one Reider had left behind him. There were perhaps eighty huts on stilts, and several stores. Parked alongside one of the huts sat a beatup 1958 cargo truck. When he saw the truck, Reider felt he was on his way home, less than an hour, two at most, depending on how fast the truck would travel. The thought thrilled him. Xuan San took him to meet the head man of the village, who shook his hand enthusiastically and assured him there were no VC present, nor anywhere in the vicinity.

They ate and talked. Xuan San told Reider that the driver of the truck was loading the vehicle with articles to deliver to a town in the south, and that they would be leaving after noon. Barring the unforseen, Reider would be let off in the town and he would be near American troops. Xuan San suggested that Reider hide in the bottom of the truck in case the VC stopped it.

Reider thanked him for his assistance, and relaxed beside a hut near the head man's quarters to wait.

It was a good day, bright with sunshine, and a cool breeze passed through the village as he lay by the hut and thought of steak and potatoes and a beautiful girl in an ao-dai. He could see himself, wearing a pressed uniform, flying over Tokyo. He would lie on a beach by the sea, and he would watch movies and go to the best restaurants. It was indeed a beautiful day.

Around one o'clock he ate again. At two the head man arrived to tell Reider that, unfortunately, the man who owned the truck had been unable to get it loaded in time, and they would have to wait until the following day for departure. The man would not drive at night. Reider was deeply disappointed, but he was not worried. He lay beside the hut the rest of the afternoon, and slept comfortably that night. Freedom lay just around the corner.

The next morning a villager woke him, and he followed the man out to the truck and crawled into the back with two or three natives. There were three tins of gas, and several malodorous packages. He crawled in amongst them. The engine clattered, the driver meshed the gears, and the truck jerked into motion.

They crawled through the village and down a rain-rutted trail to a hard-surface road, where they turned right and proceeded north, bouncing along at thirty miles an hour. Reider was still unsure as to his location. The head man of the village had refused to disclose the precise location. He was probably just overly protective of his people.

The truck rattled on, climbing steadily, and as Reider observed the terrain, he concluded that they were in the central highlands, moving south. He considered bailing off the truck and making straight for the coast because that was the most direct route back, but it was a free ride, and it was easier to let someone else do his thinking for him. He was still in a state of exhaustion, and his strength had not yet fully returned to him.

The truck halted every fifteen minutes, and the

two natives riding in back jumped out and ducked into the underbrush. "Hell of a lot of piss calls," he mumbled to himself before he dozed.

Some time later, he caught a glimpse of a Highway 14 marker. Now he knew they were heading south through the highlands. He calculated they were near the Darlac Plateau and guessed their destination to be Ban Me Thuot. A string of villages bordered Highway 14; Reider counted them as they passed.

About two o'clock, just after they had gone through the eleventh village, the truck stopped. Then Reider heard the high-pitched chatter of voices in Viet. Then he heard the driver reply and then suddenly the tailgate of the truck dropped and five pajama-clad VC jumped in and pointed submachineguns at him and ordered him out.

Numbly, he obeyed and jumped down off the truck. One of the VC marched the driver of the truck and the two natives over to the side of the road and shot them. Then he came back, gunbarrel smoking, and ordered Reider into another truck which was filled with ammunition cases. Two of the VC got into the cab of the truck, but the other three sat in the back, staring at Reider. None of them spoke. They rode for what seemed like hours until the truck came to a halt and the VC pulled Reider off and shoved him into a hut, where two guards were stationed in front.

A guard came in late in the afternoon as the sun was setting, threw some food on the floor, and left a bowl of water. Reider had no appetite, though he

knew he should eat, as that was the only chance he
had. He had to keep on eating and try to get away
again. He figured he was still somewhere in the
plateau, and from the way the VC truck had been
heading, he was not too far from the coast, perhaps fifty miles from Nha Trang. If he could
escape again, he was confident he could make it to
the coast highway and link up with an American
unit. So he waited, and lay at the open doorway
and watched the movement in the village.

He was in the village for another day, and then
he was moved again by the truck to another village
not far away. Here he was shoved underground,
through a series of tunnels, cluttered with stacked
weapons and ammunition, two hospital beds and a
large quantity of medical supplies. He guessed the
installation to be a small field hospital for the VC.

A day later three guards entered, hauled him to
his feet and dragged him up out of the tunnel into
the hut, and then out the front entrance into the
main street of the village. The sun was very bright,
and Reider thought it was about ten o'clock in the
morning. The villagers were walking back and
forth. Some stared at him, but most of them stared
at a GAZ-67B Soviet field car that was parked in
the center of the compound. Sitting in the car
were two men in North Vietnamese uniform.

"Good morning, Sergeant," called Major Lim.

Lim got out of the field car and walked over to
where Reider was standing between two VC
guards.

"You are a troublesome pet to find,"Lim continued without waiting for Reider to respond. "It is lucky for me that in your travels you were seen by some of our, shall we say, sympathizers? But it is most remarkable, Sergeant, that you managed to walk and run and get as far as you did. You amaze me. But now I have you back again, and we will have to begin your training from the first. But this time I will make sure that you do not get away."

Lim spoke to the guards, who shoved Reider into the back seat of the field car. One guard sat beside him with a pistol in his hand. Lim got into the front, spoke to the driver, and the car pulled out of the village.

They drove east along Highway 21 toward the coast, and Lim kept up a running monologue aimed at Reider. Occasionally laughing, he seemed to be having a good time.

They turned off the highway at Duc My, and stopped the field car in a village beyond. Lim left Reider with two guards and went into a hut. When he came out, he was dressed in peasant's clothes, but Reider could see the butt of his service pistol protruding from his shirt. The two guards shoved Reider into the hut and Lim followed.

"We will get you some new clothes, Sergeant," he said. "You could use a new wardrobe."

Lim pointed to a pile of black pajamas stacked on the floor.

"Find something to fit you, and be quick about it, Sergeant. We are going to take a little vacation, together, you and I, and I think you would like a change of scenery. This is an important vacation for me, because I have a very important package to deliver. And thanks to your wonderful American aircraft I do not quite trust the air. So we are going to use a little different way. Hurry up."

Reider stripped his old clothing and found a pair of the black pajamas that fitted him. He picked up a pair of sandals in the far corner of the hut and put them on. Lim leaned in the doorway as he studied Reider.

"Very good, Sergeant," he said. "If we could do something about your Caucasian face, you might almost look like a human being. And not an imperialist pig!" He struck Reider across the face. "Come along, now. I am going to give you a demonstration in combat efficiency."

CHAPTER TWENTY-THREE

With the swift silence of jungle creatures, Lim's two reinforced batallions moved through the darkness to their assigned positions, stalkers on the trail of their prey. Their dry-run rehearsals were in the process of paying off for the NVA and VC troops.

Reider watched the troops and grunted in grudging admiration. These were not the half-trained irregulars he had seen panic at the first unexpected occurrence. These NVA stalwarts were the studiously trained regulars, and they would perform in the field as such. Reider felt an ice pocket of fear form in the pit of his stomach as he thought of the sleeping artillerymen in the camp below. He knew that in a short while death would rage fiercely among them, and there was nothing he could do to prevent it. He was gagged securely, and his hands were tied.

The NVA mortar and rocket crews silently lined up on the firing stakes; they were pre-set with correct azimuths and elevations, so that the crews would be able to strike their assigned targets without needing to see where the rounds fell in the camp below. As an added safeguard, Lim had assigned separate fire control observers for each of the mortar and rocket crews. Below them, in the surrounding treeline, the infantry and special assault units made last-minute checks of their weapons and equipment. The sappers sat alone, waiting to hurl themselves upon the barbed-wire barricades of the camp with the crudely fashioned bangalore torpedoes—long hollow tubes of bamboo packed with plastic explosives. The waiting snappers lovingly fondled the tubes they would use to blast through the wire and mines, despite the fact that the tubes often would destroy their bodies with the obstacles.

The diversionary unit had inched to within two hundred meters of the camp entrance, where they silently dug shallow foxholes and cut gun positions into the earth. There they waited.

Lim made his way from his observation post to

the trench where Reider and his guard squatted, and seated himself on the edge of the trench. The major looked down upon the camp, smiling. An occasional flicker of light flashed toward them from the quiet compound as a sentry sneaked a smoke or a door opened and closed.

Lim spoke. "Do not lose patience, Reider. Enjoy the tension that we, even as enemies, have experienced many times before. Do you not find it odd that your feelings are identical not only to ours, but to those you felt before killing your enemies?"

Reider turned his head stiffly to face Lim, but the darkness hid the features of the face silhouetted in the shadows.

Reider growled. He wanted to slide a bayonet into Lim's guts. Slide it in low so it'd take hours for him to die.

Lim gave a short laugh, seized the choke collar that encircled Reider's neck and gave it a quick, vicious twist, cutting off Reider's breath. Holding the choke collar in his fist, Lim drew Reider close to his face.

"The thing I like best about you, Sergeant," Lim hissed, "is that you never let your reason rule your emotions. Before our journey together is finished, you will respect your superiors—you and all your fat, soft brethren down below us. Those swine will die in their own swill tonight. You are through, Reider. Your empire is crumbling. Do you not read the news? The day comes soon when America will sink into its own slime and strangle as you

strangle now! I rejoice. Asia's day is dawning. And
we will rise in our hundreds of millions and repay
you of the west for your centuries of exploitation.
I hate you! I despise the white skin of your bodies;
soon it will disappear from our land." Lim paused,
then went on. "And I will break you, Reider. Your
insolence will wane with your strength. This is my
time now; you belong to me."

Lim's body rocked convulsively as he released
his hold on the collar and, as the NVA officer slipped toward him with a message, rose slowly from
the blackness of the trench. Lim huddled briefly
with the messenger and returned to Reider, hiss-
ing. "Watch, and witness the slaughter of your
comrades."

Lim raised a flare gun straight above him and
fired a single green flare into the inky night.

The flare rose high into the darkness and burst
in an emerald meteor over the valley.

Abruptly the hills and trees erupted in a language of anguish and death as the long, chattering
echoes of Russian light machineguns stabbed and
stitched their 750 rounds per minute into the
sleeping fire base. The dull, resonant thump of
fifty mortars announced the shells that arced high
in the innocent night, marking it with fiery trails
from the charges on their fins. The heavier and
throatier rockets hurled whining into the camp
below. Havoc reigned in a rage of destruction.
Reider's eyes turned from the scene below to the
face of a grinning, maniacal Lim, whose own eyes
were riveted on the scene below.

Dazed and terrified GIs staggered and ran from their blazing quarters into the raging fury of the machinegun mortar fire.

"From frying pan to the fire, eh, Reider?" Lim taunted him.

Reider muttered in reply.

Lim laughed. "I see you like the show I have provided for your entertainment."

As the shrieking rounds struck the fuel dumps below, volcanoes roared forth in the night, belching high columns of fire and oily smoke that seemed to blacken the night itself. Men ran madly, flaming ants in panic, their clothing ablaze. The night was alive with screams of pain underneath the rain of molten death. A concentrated barrage of rocket and mortar fire fell upon the buildings in a furious deluge; flaming hunks of metal and flesh were hurled end over end through the night.

Lim's diversionary force attacked from the gate, sending long, level streams of machinegun fire across the camp. The steady, traversing fire raked the fire base in repeating patterns. Then came the crackling, sporadic sputter of small arms as fifty NVA laid down seemingly endless chains of fire, loading and re-loading rapidly as they emptied hot chambers of death. GIs were scrambling in T-shirts and shorts to counteroffensive positions.

Lim grinned. NVA mortar rounds now began a slow and steady walk through the wire and mines on the southern edge of the camp and into the center of the fire base, pounding the installation with an absorbed concentration.

VC sappers raced forward to throw their bangalore torpedoes into the remaining wire barricades,
followed by Lim's assault forces, who rushed into
the opening created by the fanatical sappers, hurt-
ling the punji stake ditch and entering the compound.

But then the base's deadly claymores were
detonated electrically, each packet of explosive
sending seven hundred steel balls into the assault
forces. And Reider relished each death among the
NVA. It looked as if the onslaught would fail:
twisted bodies flopped, smoking, into the wire.
But then Lim's reserve units rushed forward,
pouring into the gap with roars of frenzy, their
SKS's and Kalashnikov AK 47 rifles cutting into
the GIs.

Reider moaned as two U.S. artillery positions
were knocked out before they fired a single round.
But then he saw an American rally four men to
him, seize an M60 machinegun, drop into the
81mm mortar pit and begin to hose down the NVA
who ran through the gap, directing his fire with
tracer ball ammo, severing legs from wave after
wave of NVA as they raced through the wire. Then
the men got the mortar working, and they began to
throw round after furious round into the treeline
from which the NVA was still streaming. The
81mm shells shattered among the NVA, tossing
bodies like broken toys into the erupting night.

Even as the men loaded and fired with super-
human speed, an NVA officer and six subordinates
leapt into the mortar pit, killing two Americans

with long bursts from their AK47s.

The grizzled machinegunner whirled, turning his weapon on the NVA behind him, too late to prevent the stab wound from the NVA nearest him.

The gunner grabbed the smaller Viet by the throat and squeezed with a grip of death. The two toppled backward, the sergeant's mouth open in a silent scream never uttered, and the Viet a broken puppet.

The two remaining raised their hands in surrender, only to be cut down and stabbed repeatedly by the Viets. Reider buried his face in his arms and sobbed uncontrollably.

Throughout the compound, NVA squads ran from position to position, tossing satchel charges and grenades into burning bunkers and barracks. Hysteria seized the NVA troops as they ran, screaming cries of ultimate victory. The incongruous shout of, "Ho Chi Minh was a pimp!" caused Reider to jerk his head sharply and search the smoking compound for the owner of that defiant voice.

Beyond the burning commo room, Reider could see an American gather men into two machinegun bunkers that were connected with a trench line. And as the leader shouted insults at the NVA, he signalled for his men to open fire. Abruptly, in sporadic bursts that soon assumed a steady rate of fire, the surviving Americans poured .30 and .50 caliber shells into the Viets. The Viet troops charged, regrouped and charged again.

Time was of the essence to the combatants. Both the besieged Americans and the attacking Viets were aware of the fact that a reconnaissance flight would soon be ordered to find out why the fire base had not observed its hourly check-in. This inspired the few remaining Americans to fight on and infuriated the Viets, goading them into even more frenzied charges. The fire base was yet to be taken.

Lim began to bark furious orders, sending runners with hurried instructions into the camp below. Reider smiled, his hope rising for those Americans yet alive. If only he could live to witness the terrible vengeance wreaked upon the NVA when the reaction units reached the scene.

Lim slammed his binoculars to the ground, shrieked at Reider's guard to bring his prisoner along, and then slowly descended to the battle scene that raged in the camp below, the guard following, holding the choke leash that led Reider in tow.

Lim stopped at a wall of sandbags when a six-round burst of machinegun fire struck the three NVA in front of him. He dropped to his knees; Reider's guard pulled him into an abandoned gun position and pressed a gun barrel to his temple. A second six-round burst ripped into the ragged wall of sandbags.

More calmly than Reider had expected, Lim began to take control of his units, directing first one and then another with a disciplined professionalism.

Turning to his radioman, Lim ordered his observer crews to lay down fire on the two hold-out bunkers, directing them to fire long and then walk the rounds in to their targets.

Lim laughed triumphantly as he observed the mortar rounds screeching into the targeted area, and suddenly, in a fit of frenzy, ordered his troops to charge into their own murderous fire. But to no avail. The Cong flattened themselves upon the ground. Grazing fire from the American-held bunkers roared over the heads of the prone Viets.

Lim ran from one occupied position to another, cursing and kicking his men, screaming orders to move.

The NVA began to rise and move forward. Lim shoved and pushed and pummelled his men until they were all moving straight into the savage machinegun fire. Two Viets broke ranks and turned to run, their eyes wide with terror, only to be met with Lim's pistol fire. Even as they fell, shot through the head, Lim snatched a satchel charge from one of the dead deserters and ran toward the nearest bunker, waving to his men to follow him as he pulled the fuse cord with his teeth and threw it at the target he had chosen, diving to the ground behind a pile of dead American and Viet bodies.

The satchel charge exploded within the bunker, killing most of the Americans inside. To a man, Lim's troops rushed into the smoking structure to shoot and bayonet the wounded.

"One yet alive!" yelled Lim. "Finish the foolish

filthy dog!"

Now all the Viets, excited to an insanity beyond caution, charged pell-mell into the fire of the machineguns that were levelled at them from the east wall. Their ranks torn apart, they regrouped and surged toward the bunker again.

Suddenly the machinegun stopped. As the American inside the bunker strove feverishly to clear his jammed weapon, the NVA overran his position. The corporal threw himself to the floor of the bunker and pulled the pins of two hand grenades as the NVA poured in upon him. The bunker blew up in a blinding white flash of phosphorus as the grenades ignited stored mortar shells.

The roar shook the earth of the compound, and Reider rose to see fragments of metal and flesh meld in mid-air with white-hot bits of phosphorus that seared their way across the camp like miniature meteors. Those outside the bunker who were wounded ran screaming as the burning white coals bored through flesh and bone.

Lim turned to an aide and ordered that his wounded men be removed at once, but there was yet one position left to be taken and he was preparing for a new assault.

Across the grounds, now strewn with the dead and debris, Reider could see the Americans gather themselves for battle in a bunker beside the gate. To his left, Reider watched Lim muster his NVA, snapping orders, struggling to rally them for the final, decisive assault.

Sickened at the slaughter, Reider nevertheless felt an immense satisfaction that Lim had thus far failed to attain his objective. More than two hundred NVA lay dead or wounded. With any luck, Reider thought, the compound would be U.S. territory come sunup. If they could just hold. . . .

The NVA charge began.

With cries of hatred the NVA streamed across the camp ground, hurling their grenades thoughtlessly, long before they were in effective range, a great crush of packed bodies in berserk attack.

An 81mm mortar roared from the bunker, an American NCO yelled, "Surprise," and the captain fired three illuminating rounds. As the flares rose high and broke over the camp, the Viets halted, stumbling. The sudden brilliance had blinded them. The captain ordered his men to open fire on the closely packed bodies of the NVA.

Dozens of NVA and VC fell.

Lim drove them on, shrieking his fury. They lurched and blundered forward, over the bodies of the fallen.

As Lim shot those of his troops who dared balk, Reider heard a new sound: the throb of helicopters. After a moment the Viet ranks heard it, too. Abruptly, they broke and ran, scattering in as many directions as there were men.

Major Lim's screams of rage could not be heard over the chopachopachopa of the approaching helicopters, and though Lim tried to give chase as his men fled, there was nothing he could do. Turning, Lim ran to the wall of sandbags where he had left his prisoner, grabbed the choke collar and snarled, "This is a matter for which you must atone, Sergeant!"

And with a savage yank on the leash, Lim began to jog out of the compound and through the jungle, tugging Reider after him as the guard brought up the rear.

Overhead, U.S. Air Force jets streaked from the sky to strafe the fleeting Viets with machinegun and rocket fire, cannons blasting at the retreating Viets even as the napalm plastered the twisting paths with flames.

Lim halted at the rise of ground that overlooked the valley, turned and shoved Reider into the undergrowth and then sought cover himself. Reider's guards had deserted.

And from his place of hiding, Lim watched his men race in mindless flight as U.S. jet aircraft attacked with napalm.

Lim ground his teeth as he watched his men disintegrate and vowed eternal vengeance. Then he cursed his men for their having faltered.

Reider mumbled a prayer of thankfulness that he had been allowed to witness Lim's humiliation.

The jets were still roaring back and forth over the fields, picking off NVA as though they were mice. Reider laughed, because it was good.

CHAPTER TWENTY-FOUR

Day broke indifferently. Molten bursts still rain-
ed upon the NVA and VC as the fear-stricken
troops streamed toward the jungle. Lim raced ahead
of his men momentarily, in an effort to escape the
merciless rain, but Reider could not sustain the
furious pace, stumbling and sprawling headlong
in a tangle of arms and legs with Lim. The NVA
raced around them, indifferent to their fallen
leader. Lim jerked Reider to his aching feet, jerked
at the leather thong, and rejoined the race for

cover. An animal mindlessness permeated the
ranks of NVA troops. They fled en masse, throwing weapons away in an entanglement of panic as
they sped toward the security of the trees, aban-
doning stragglers to the automatic fire that stalked
them. Survival was of the essence.

Lim trailed after his men, clutching the leash
that held Reider, eyes disbelieving, body rigid,
hurrying with short, jerky movements. Convulsive
shudders coursed his small frame.

In the camp, as the copters landed, they discharged the dreaded Yards, who raced across the
compound killing all the Viets in their path. The
hurried intervention of Williams' Special Forces
cadre alone prevented the hillmen from killing all
the wounded. Four NVA were taken alive. Terrified of the savage Montagnards, they abruptly told
all they knew. Thus Williams learned of the American POW whom Major Lim held captive and
treated so insanely. The destruction that had be-
fallen the Fire Base was indication enough of
Lim's fanaticism. A thick stillness descended upon
the field installation. The dead lay contorted,
broken, hands outstretched, grasping at nothing,
as though they could cling to life itself. The smells
of cordite and smoke clung to the dead as posses-
sively as carrion crows.

Sizemore and Williams looked at one another,
then walked slowly away from the Viet prisoners.

Montagnards gathered around the Viet prisoners. The ensuing silence was broken only by the

deep, even breathing of the men. Then the Yards drew their bayonets, and the short, machete-like bush knives they had made in their home villages. As they drew closer, with a cry coming from deep within them, the blades began to swing. . . .

After two minutes, Williams called the Strikers in, loading them back into the choppers. Somewhere close an American was being led away on a leash like a dog. They were going to find him. They had to intercept the Viets before they crossed the Dap Rao River, only fifteen miles away, and entered Cambodia. They had known about a Cong crossing of the Dap Rao for months; today they'd use it for a good kill.

The Viets streamed into the underbrush, breaking into smaller groups and then reassembling, disoriented. They moved through the valley in knots and struggling clots, stumbling along through the clutching claws of undergrowth.

Overhead, the high-pitched whine of U.S. fighter bombers assailed their ears. The menacing jets laid down steams of fire at all movements, driving the NVA into panic. The NVA pushed on, determined to claw their way to safety behind the border ahead of them.

Lim had gradually gained control of himself, gathering around him a unit of fourteen men to whom he spoke reassuringly, sending them out to do the same for the retreating battalions, to calm the men, to stop their blind flight. Slowly the panic-stricken infantry began to respond. They formed into larger functioning units of twenty and thirty men, heading to the Dap Rao River.

In the sky above, the fighters lost contact with the fleeing Viets, but still the jets circled, expending their remaining ammunition at any likely spot.

Some of them scored lucky hits, but not many.

The gunboats and troop-carrying Huey helicopters carried the Special Forces Mike Force over the retreating Viets and set them down on the South Vietnam side of the Dap Rao. The choppers took off, other units would wait on standby for radio communication from the Mike Force that the North Viets were at the crossing. Then they would then return and give fire support to the ground forces.

Williams looked at Sizemore, then at the river. Size nodded his head, smiled, and motioned their troops to follow. They waded the waist-deep water to the Cambodian side. After all, they would be fools not to catch the enemy wide open and exposed in a river crossing.

The Special Forces advisors began to position their men quickly, digging in and camouflaging their positions, setting light machineguns on both flanks so they could have interlocking fire at the river's center. The tiger-striped camouflage suits of the Strikers blended perfectly into the shadows.

After all was set, Sizemore and Williams crossed the river to see what their positions looked like from the Viet side. Everything was in order. Noth-

ing showed that two companies of savage Montagnard tribesmen lay in wait. Satisfied, the SF men
rejoined their troops.

Williams knew that the Viets were still at least
three or four hours away. His unit was heavily
outnumbered, but the Viets would be exhausted
and thirsty by the time they reached the crossing.
That and the element of surprise should throw the
odds in his favor—and having those Cobra gun-
ships standing by wouldn't hurt things a damn
bit, either. So they waited.

The sun climbed high in the trees, bringing the
heat of midday.

And they waited.

As the hours passed, Reider's throat grew raw
with thirst, his shirt streaked with white from the
salty sweat which had soaked through and dried.
But there would be no water until they reached
the river. What water the Viets had had in can-
teens had long since been drunk. Fear is a thirsty
business.

They moved toward the river.

Williams once again looked at his positions,
trying to put himself in the Viets' state of mind.
What would they do when they reached the river
bank? Would they attempt a crossing immediately, or would they wait on the Vietnam side and
cross as a unit? Better safe than dead. He gave new
orders to the Montagnards, to move back, form-

ing a pocket on the Cambodian side, a pocket fifty
yards wide at the river bank and forty yards deep,
providing plenty of room for a number of Viet
troops to cross the river without waiting for the
rest of their units. Those that did cross would
stop, for once they reached the Cambodian side
they would be safe, wouldn't they? After all, this
was neutral territory, and the Americans were not
allowed to cross over. Here they would wait for
the rest of their comrades to catch up. After all
they had gone through they would be exhausted.
Well, the SF captain had something to help them
rest.

He called the Yard CO and whispered to him. A
few minutes later the Yard returned with what
looked like a suitcase. Williams opened it. Inside
were three unAmerican submachineguns, Swedish Ks. Each had a strange-looking attachment for
the barrel—a specially built silencer. The only
sound that would be heard from these weapons as
they fired their special 9mm subsonic rounds
would be the bolt slapping back and forth, not a
sound that would carry across the river.

Williams smiled. These pieces had been expensive, very expensive—five cases of Cutty Sark and
three of Jim Beam. Big Jay had bartered them
from a Spook heading up to Long Vinh, then on to
Laos. After all, it got pretty dry on the Plaine Des
Jarres.

Three of his bodyguard Strikers had been trained in their use; Williams gave the weapons to them
now, with instructions to take out any Viets that

came to close to the camouflaged positions of his Strike Force. One K would be used on each of the three sides forming the pocket of the banks of Dap Rao.

CHAPTER TWENTY-FIVE

The first of the Viets reached the Dap Rao, emerging slowly from the jungle, bodies shaking with fatigue, uniforms streaked with lines of dark sweat. These first few stopped briefly on the Vietnam side, lowered their faces into the brown, running waters, and drank. The Americans and Yards watched as the first arrivals sat back and rested, looking peacefully around them. Then a number of them left the rest and began wading through the waist-deep waters. Once across, they lay down on the banks, looking back at their comrades on the opposite bank, relief manifesting itself in the too-loud way they talked. They were safe. Less than half had their weapons with them, but they were safe now, and would be rearmed later. As they rested, more and more of the retreating Viets straggled in. Slowly a crowd gathered on the Vietnamese bank, and as more NVA officers and noncoms arrived they began whipping the men into ranks, not permitting them to cross the river without orders.

Williams' radioman made contact with the Cobra gunboats. Contact was acknowledged. The gunboats were coming.

The approximately forty Viets on the Cambodian side of the river studied the events taking place opposite them. Major Lim was not there. He was at the rear, whipping stragglers on.

The officers at last assembled their men into a semblance of order and began the crossing.

As they waded into the murky waters of the Dap Rao, the Mike Force on the Cambodian side prepared themselves.

The Viets who had crossed earlier moved to the river bank, ready to help their exhausted comrades, bunching together as they came across. Williams raised his hand, pointed to the three Yards with the silenced Swedish Ks, pointed to the bunched-up NVA, and slashed the air. The three silenced Ks went to work, sending in less than seven seconds ninety 9mm bullets into the backs of the tightly grouped Viets.

They fell in pairs, then threes, wounded, dead before their bodies dropped upon the bank.

The captain's hand slashed the air a second time, signaling the 60mm mortar crews. The lobbing rounds throbbed into the river among the crossing Viets. Great fountains of water rose from the Dap Rao.

Simultaneously, Sizemore opened fire with an M60 light machinegun, and a barrage of small-arms fire from the two Yard companies followed, sweeping across the targeted area like a scythe, cutting Viets into shreds in a murderous crossfire that raged through the center of the river again and again.

The Strikers moved forward to the bank and began throwing pineapples as rapidly as they could pull the pins, pitching them into the murky waters, where they exploded with dull whumps that blew huge gouts of water skyward, filling the air with a bloody mist as the blood from dying Viets mingled with the chocolate waters of the Dap Rao.

Near hysteria, most of the living Vietnamese in the river turned, churning their way toward the bank they had left, while others dove under water to escape, only to be blown to the surface as more grenades exploded in the Dap Rao.

Overhead, gunboats and eight helicopters swung into action, spewing leaden death into the Vietnamese bank of the Dap Rao, where waiting Viets tried to cover the withdrawal of their comrades with what firepower they could muster. It was not enough. The choppers drove them back into the jungle wall and away from their buddies. Four of the gunboats turned their attention to those still in the river, joining their fire with that of the Strikers, sending wave after wave of machinegun fire and rockets into the struggling bodies.

They finished their last pass four minutes after the first round had been fired—four minutes of death that bent time out of proportion. It had seemed like hours—and for some it had been even longer. Eternity had reached out for over two hundred and fifty NVA and VC.

When Lim heard the sound of gunfire ahead of him and saw the shadows of the gunboats passing above the mottled green canopy of jungle, he knew what was taking place: his men were being ambushed and cut to ribbons. Without hesitating, Lim turned and headed further north. There was an alternate crossing five miles up the river. The stragglers that had gathered around him had eyes wide with fear. Lim looked at Reider for a moment as if he were going to say something, turned away and led the way in silence. Reider saw the expression in Lim's eyes: Lim had reached the limit of his tolerances.

Williams and Sizemore quit firing, a light blue smoke coming from their overheated weapons. They stood and moved to the bank. In front of them, the bodies of the enemy lay on their faces in the river being pulled by the current, slowly turning as the waters carried them south. The Strikers joined them, waiting for orders. Williams signaled them to cross, wading back across the Dap Rao to Vietnam, pushing drifting bodies aside, not bothering to see if all were dead. The river would take care of any that still held the spark of life.

The captain ordered that prisoners be taken; the rage he had felt at the fire base had been purged from him. But only those with a chance of living were taken. The badly wounded were given to the river, an easier death than lying on the banks of the Dap Rao for hours waiting for their end.

The SF men hunted among the dead and wounded for any sign of the American. No luck. He wasn't to be found.

Sizemore cursed wearily and turned to Williams: "Well at least the poor bastard was alive a couple of hours ago. Maybe we'll be able to put something together from what the prisoners tell us. With your permission I'll let Jaw talk to one or two of them when we get back."

Williams wiped his face with the back of a grimy hand and grimaced. Jaw was a Bihnar tribesman so named for his heavy jawbones and oversized teeth. When they had a prisoner who wouldn't talk, Jaw would somehow extract it from them when all else failed. There was never a mark on the prisoners when they were returned, though several committed suicide when threatened with a repeat visit.

Sizemore scratched his short pepper-grey hair and looked at the wall of the jungle, silently wish-

ing the captured GI out there somewhere a quick
and easy death. He turned and went back to the
business at hand. Another action was over, and
this one had worked for them. Time to go home
and wait again for another call. Perhaps the next
time they wouldn't be so lucky. They had lost only
eight men dead and eleven wounded, and most of
the wounded would make it. Well, shit, thought
the sergeant, only two more months and I could be
heading home away from all this. But I know I'm
not going to make it back, not yet. Well, what's one
more extension? I got no wife and the kids are
grown and don't give a damn about me. I might as
well stay around. I know Williams isn't going
back. Not now, without word about Reider.

Lim and his stragglers worked their way north
along the twisting trail to the alternate crossing,
Lim in a quiet fury, building his hate every time he
looked at what was left of his men. As they moved
through the brush, a whipping branch slapped the
still tender stump of Lim's aputated arm, sending
a cold, searing pain shooting to his spine and
brain. Lim gave a short, curt groan. The pain cleared his mind, and he seemed to draw strength from
it. Strength and hate. He could feel Reider's eyes
on him, watching, gloating over his losses. Reider.
The smug swine! He'd teach him who the master
was when they reached the village. He would
teach Reider who was master in this land.

As they struggled on, Reider's mind wandered,
to try and isolate itself from the burning cramps

in his back and neck, the cracked lips that bled and stung, but always his thoughts returned to Lim. How much longer before it would end? He was not as strong as before. Near starvation had weakened him almost to his limits. Now he must walk lightly, wait his time, rest, try to gain strength, and then try again. What had happened today gave him hope, but he also knew what it had done to Lim. Lim would be more dangerous than ever before. So he would watch and wait, watch and wait.

He'd done it once. With luck he could do it again. Watch. And wait.

CHAPTER TWENTY-SIX

Outside the village of Prey Veng, on the bank of the Srepok River, Lim called a halt and ordered his men to straighten themselves up as much as possible. Then he lectured them, assuring them that victory would have been theirs had it not been for the helicopters and bombers, consoling them that they had in fact beaten the Americans, and that they should take great pride in their accomplishment. He urged them to enter the village as victors and not "beaten dogs."

Reider observed that Lim failed to mention the facts that his troops had broken before the air strike had arrived, and that his men had run before the concentrated fire of the surviving Americans.

Lim talked on, slowly beginning to believe his own story that they had "won."

The NVA troops, Lim at their head, entered the village of Prey Veng like victors. Reider smiled.

Apparently Lim was determined to rebuild his regiment. Here he would regroup his forces, take the surviving men, and spread them throughout the recruits being sent from the south.

Reider was locked into a suspended cage, much like the one he'd been in before, and then Lim ignored him, busy with the job of training the new volunteers sent to him by VC recruiters.

Reider watched the endless drills, noting that army drills were the same anywhere in the world —except that in Lim's unit any recruit who did not give his utmost was made to understand the errors of his ways in a number of unforgettable Special Training Exercises, or in public execution for lack of the proper revolutionary spirit.

Reider watched the endless drills, losing himself in his own mind for hours, recalling his own training, the men he had trained. How many of his old group were left? Where were they now? It was difficult for him to recall faces, but with his eyes closed the voices came through clearly to him. Still, he simply could not attach the right faces to the voices he could hear clearly.

The days were long as he squatted rocking back and forth, no longer even trying to brush the flies from his face—a face that aged and furrowed; the skin toughened, growing stiff as parchment.

And still Reider waited and watched. Time. He had all the time in the world.

Occasionally Lim would bring the new volunteers to see Reider. Lim would point to him as an example of what Americans were really like. "Nothing but animals of the lowest kind," Lim would swear.

On special occasions Lim had the guards take Reider from his cage, help him to his feet, strip him naked and blindfold him. Then he would have Reider pushed naked from man to man in a circle of howling faces that Reider could not see, a circle of laughing Oriental faces that would spit on him, faces that Reider never knew but longed to smash. Beatings, isolation, starvation—this humiliation was the worst yet: to be naked before his enemies. A mere loincloth assumed colossal importance to him; if only he had that shield to protect himself from their mocking laughter and their contempt.

Reider would almost find himself asking Lim—no, begging Lim—to stop. But he didn't. His mind continued to reassure him that it would end, that all things end in time, that this was not really happening to him, that it was happening to someone else. And then the circle of horror would stop and they would drag him through the village back to his cage, the red dust filling his mouth, caking his skin, and hardening in great, filthy scabs in his hair. Back to his cage. And he waited.

One night a cool wind told of yet another monsoon season's approach. Reider shivered as the breeze evaporated the day's residue of sweat. He waited for the rains.

They came. First, a blowing cloud of dust across the village, then the first drops that increased until it seemed as though the sky had broken. And in this rain Reider put his arms around his knees, holding them tight to his chest for whatever feeble warmth he could get from his own body. He waited and watched, tensing and flexing his legs, rubbing his calves, hoping to be ready when the time came. And he waited.

How long had passed? Three months? Four? It no longer mattered. But now Lim had finished the training of his new battalions, and soon Lim would have time for him again.

The night came moonless—and still the rain fell. Across the clearing in a long house several young Viets celebrated becoming full-fledged members of the People's Army of Liberation, drinking homemade rice wine. With every swallow they became more convinced of their own courage.

Reider's guard sat inside with them, out of the rain, and dozed. What need was there to stand out in the rain? The American was not going anywhere, and it had been a long day. The guard had eaten heavily of rice and roast pig that day, and he dozed.

Soon one of the young Viets went to the door of the long house and vomited, and as he raised his

head his eyes caught sight of Reider's cage swinging gently in the wind. "The American dog! Hai!"
He would show his comrades how he could master
the Americans.

The drunken young Viet straggered to the cage,
cursing softly in the rain. He looked at Reider
through the bamboo bars. So this was the enemy?
There was nothing to fear from beasts like this.
Why, he had played with him, laughed at his shriv-
eled manhood, and the animal had cringed. There
was no fight in this paper tiger. Had he not seen
the children of the village spit on him? No real
man of pride and honor would take such treat-
ment. A real man would kill himself first. He
would take this piece of filth back to the long
house for the amusement of his noble comrades.

The young Viet moved closer to the bars, looked
up at Reider and spat into Reider's face. The spittle struck Reider's cheek and ran down his face
slowly.

Reider did not move. He had no idea why the
drunken young fool was there. Wait. Wait while
the drunken youth pulls at the cage to open it. But
Lim has the key.

The Viet stopped in confusion. So the cage
would not open. Well, he was tired anyway and
one of the young women of the village had looked
upon him with smiling eyes today. He would find
her. He turned from the cage and slipped, falling
back against the bars of the cage. Before Reider
knew it, his own hands had reached through the
bamboo bars and grabbed the Viet by the throat,

his thumbs digging deep into the base of the neck
while his fingers tightened around the neck,
squeezing and pulling.

The Viet's body went into a long, trembling
spasm, and as the pressure mounted in his brain, a
single thought passed through the red mist pulling
him down: No! No! Please! No! And he died,
Reider hanging on and shaking, refusing to let go,
all the hate rising into his throat and releasing itself in an animal cry.

Reider threw back his head and screamed, the
muscles in his arms and hands sending every
ounce of his strength into his fingers till they
broke through the skin of the Viet's neck and tore
into the flesh beneath. Reider screamed with
every bit of life in him.

The camp grew quiet. Not a sound came from
the dimly lit long houses. Then Reider's guard
dashed out, and saw his prisoner holding a dead
Viet and screaming through the rain and tears
that streamed down his face. The guard ran and
began smashing Reider's face with the rifle butt,
slamming his blows between the bars until
Reider's face was a bloody pulp. Still Reider
screamed from deep in his guts, a sound that only
a soul in torment could release.

Lim awoke to the cries from outside, realized at
once that it was Reider, drew his pistol and ran to
the cage, where Reider, his face bloody, still held
the dead Viet and screamed through his broken
face.

Reider's screaming stopped when he saw Lim.

His fingers relaxed, letting the dead Viet fall to the ground.

Lim looked at the wet, limp body, then at Reider. He took the key from his pants pocket and ordered the guard to open the cage. A number of soldiers and villagers gathered near, watching as Lim ordered two men to pull Reider from his cage.

Lim looked upon Reider, held before him by the two men, his face horrible.

"Sergeant Reider, I have had enough from you," Lim hissed. "You still think that someday you will escape. Or that the war will end and you will be sent home. Listen to me. You will not fight me anymore. You are never going to leave me."

Lim snapped a short order to the Viets and they threw Reider to the ground and raised his feet chest high. Lim reached across, pulled a bayonet from the scabbard on one of the guards, and with two long, steady strokes he severed the Achilles' tendon in each of Reider's legs.

"From this day forward, Sergeant," said Lim as he returned the bayonet to its scabbard, "you will be able to crawl much faster than you can run. Until the day you die, Sergeant. Now you will crawl."

CHAPTER TWENTY-SEVEN

Williams and Sizemore sat alone at the Nautique. The monsoon had come and gone. Mac had gone stateside. No one blamed him; he was the only one of them with a wife and small kids to take care of.

Williams had tried to get HQ to let them go in after the American. But they were told to keep their asses out of Cambodia; shit was still coming down on HQ from their excursion by the Dap Rao.

The prisoners they'd interrogated hadn't given

them very much to go on. They said Lim might be at a village called Prey Veng, but it wasn't on any maps. They were pretty sure the American was dead, after what the prisoners had told them about Lim. Still, they waited. For some reason— neither of them could explain it—they had become convinced that the American was Reider. He *had* to be alive. He *had* to.

A familiar shadow covered their table. Big Jay sat down. "Get your jaws off the barroom floor, boys. I got something. You know those Cambodian bandits, the Kamserai. The Company pays them off in opium and weapons to ambush Charley's supply lines and gather Intell." He lowered his voice. "They passed the word that the mother-fucker who hit the firebase is named Lim something or other and he has an American for a pet. That's what they said, a pet. Lim keeps him on a leash and treats him just as you would a damned dog or something. Any way the clincher is this, the village Lim is in is a training center called Prey Veng. Now, how does that grab your ass?"

Williams and Sizemore glowered. "Where the hell *is* Prey Veng? We don't have anything to go on other than the name, and that ain't enough. You know that!"

Jay grinned evilly and took a plastic-wrapped packet from his shirt pocket. "I spent six weeks trying to locate the place. Every time I could scrounge a few hours between missions or had enough gas after one, I took off to the area where the Kamserais said Prey Veng was located. I spotted it last week, and went back twice to make sure. Got some pictures." He opened the pack and took out a map of Cambodia and a set of photos. Sizemore took these and went over them one by one, taking his time. He told Williams, "I can make out some VC troops and what looks like a munitions depot but that's all. I'll take these back and go over them with a glass later. But there's not much doubt that this is Lim's camp. Too many things hang together." He leaned closer to Williams. "You know that even if Reider has been snuffed, we still owe him for Plei Jrong."

Williams hesitated. "How would we get in and out of there? HQ damn sure is not going to let us just take some planes or copters and go flying off into the sunset."

Jay coughed gently. "Next week I'll be making a hard rice drop—ammunition—from a C-130. If you and your people were around Holloway then, I could pick you up on my way back. In an hour I'd have you over a field you could use as a drop zone. It's less than three miles from the village."

That decided it. Williams knew it was more than likely that he'd get busted, if not forced to resign. But, as Sizemore said, even if Reider wasn't there, they still owed Lim. Payment was long overdue. He knew there'd be no problem with the Strikers. They could care less if they were in Cambodia or Albania as long as they could kill Cong and get paid for it.

"Okay. We go for it. We're supposed to be back

at Pleiku Monday anyway, and the team is already there. Jay, it's up to you, big fella.''

Jay smiled, showing teeth large enough to peel cocoanuts. "I'll be there. But once you're on the ground, how are you going to get back?"

Sizemore answered for both of them. "Walk!"

Clouds of red dust floated over the airfield at Holloway. Cooking smoke drifted over Pleiku, settling over the tin-roofed shanties and bars. Williams' Strike Force had been ready since long before dawn, standing by in an empty hanger. They had a full complement, one hundred strong.

The sentries at the airbase had long since learned not to ask too many questions about why SF types were hanging around. The Mike Force had been given a curious look and left alone.

Sizemore went over everyone's gear personally, making them lay it out, then repack under his eye. Each man carried only one ration pack. The rest of their sixty-pound load per man was ammo; only the medics carried anything else. Parachutes rested at each man's feet. They wouldn't put them on till they were in the air. It made no sense to stand around in one of those damned things for what might be hours. Size had had a message from the big guy, namely: "Time to kick ass and take names; any time from 0500 on!"

0500 came and went, as did 0800, and 1000, each hour longer than the last. It was a few minutes before 1100 when Sizemore gave a whistle for Williams to join him by the hanger door. Shading his eyes to see, Williams could just make out through the haze the lumpy shape of a C-130 coming in. The plane touched down, backed its props, and came straight in, taking the off-ramp that would lead it by the hanger where Sizemore, Williams, and the Yards were waiting. This was it! Size gave the order for everyone to get ready to move out and board the plane.

Jay dropped the tailgate and waved them on from the cockpit. The engines were kept running, throwing up clouds of the red dust, drowning out all other sounds. Once the Mike Force was strapped into their canvas seats, the huge plane turned, Jay easing off the brakes and throwing the shift to the throttles. As he had begun his approach, Jay had requested and received immediate clearance for a turnaround. The controllers at Pleiku knew that it was wise to let the Air America people have what they wanted. Those who asked too many questions could find themselves doing some very uncomfortable duty, duty that could get them shot at, far from the comfortable barracks, the bars and the women. Today they asked no questions.

Jay pulled his stick back, angling the plane higher, climbing. The throbbing of the motors settled back to a comfortable deep hum. Williams went up front to talk with Jay. Sizemore ordered the Mike Force to put on their chutes. It wouldn't be long before they'd be over the drop zone. Size lit up a cigarette, cupping his hands to shield the flame. Sucking the smoke in deep, he held it a moment, then let it out slowly. He watched his men; their dark faces were imperturable. They were like well-behaved children whose parents were taking them on a picnic. They had asked no questions, not even where they were going. Good men! He wondered what would happen to them if they lost this war. What would be the fate of those who had fought against the Cong? He didn't like to think of it, any more than he liked thinking about Reider being in the hands of Lim.

Shredding out his cigarette, he wriggled into his chute harness, adjusting the straps for the thousandth time. It always amazed him: every time he put on the damn thing, it wasn't more than five minutes before he had to take a leak.

Williams returned, nodded approvingly when he saw the men in their harnesses, weapons and gear secured. "Jay says we'll be over the drop zone in an hour and ten minutes."

Size nodded, and leaned back against the canvas webbing of his seat. There was nothing to do, except wait. The minutes always seemed to drag on for hours, until the moment came to stand up, hook up, and shuffle to the door. Then those minutes seemed like seconds.

Sizemore looked forward to rescuing Reider, if he was alive, and killing Lim.

He ran a hand through his grizzled hair. Any way it went down, when this flight was over, win, lose, or draw, he was going to pack it in. He'd had enough. Maybe there wasn't anything at home for him any more, but he knew that each day there was less for him in Vietnam or any place like it.

He was a dinosaur, long overdue his time for extinction and peace.

CHAPTER TWENTY-EIGHT

The transformation was total. Reider became the Moi, the mocked beast of Prey Veng; the filth-encrusted, shuffling creature of obeisance; a spirit—crippled piece of protoplasm that prostrated itself before the overturned bowl of rice and grovelled for the grit-caked bits of meat the villagers threw aside. Life still coursed through the tattered, bruised, and misshapen form that once had stood proudly and erect, but the life force itself now seemed to pulse in spite of those inner drives that

seemed determined to destroy him, to put an end
to the identity that was Reider. He had no cogni-
zance of these warring factions within him; he
simply whimpered and begged his way through
the village, the light of his will to live dimmed to a
small but insistent whisper. He did not know what
kept him alive. Something within him simply
would not let go.

The tortuous months of captivity had taken an
inestimable toll of him, and yet his spirit had survived. Until Lim's cutting. It was as though
Reider's very soulstuff had been sapped of its
strength by that act. He behaved like a circus
animal now, amusing the villagers with little
tricks that sprang from within him unplanned, un-
announced. His features frozen into a dirtied
facade of expressionless granite, Reider would
suddenly break into strange gyrations for scraps
and tidbits tossed to him in a way that only the
village dogs could comprehend. Nor did he snarl
when struck with stones or sticks, but merely
slunk away, completely cowed, no longer interested in retaliation.

For all practical purposes Reider had ceased to
exist. There was no longer a need to keep him
caged by day, or even a need to force him into his
cage at night, for Reider voluntarily entered his
cage before he could be ordered to do so. It had become his world, the only security to which he
could withdraw.

Even when the distant sound of aircraft engines
came from the sky, he paid no more attention to it

than he did the flies that gathered in the corners of his eyes to lay their eggs. The unseen plane was something from a world that no longer existed. Life still dwelled within the tortured and bleeding frame that was his body, but it was a life that did not know of life, a breathing shambles that was heedless of indignities, unmindful of the foulness, decay and degradation.

He felt emotion only when the villagers gathered for their periodic festival. As they beat their drums and brass gongs, the rhythm would rise and throb through the village, and Reider would nod his head in unison to the pulsing beat. The drums stirred old associations at a level deep within him. He responded, his movements scarcely perceptible at first, but then slowly gaining strength as his will groped with the mind it was determined to recover. In the darkest reaches of Reider's mind, the rat-tat-tat ran repeatedly, returning in insistent ripples. Rat-tat-tat. Again and again the rat-tat-tat beat its way through him until he could see himself as a child again, thrilled by the parade that passed before him, row on row of uniformed ranks of soldiers strode by in a stream of steel and leather, rat-tat-tat, rat-tat-tat, the rhythm muffled, then thunderous, then muffled again. The beat burned its way though his being as Reider sat and nodded, as the timeless call itself beckoned him, reminded him of another life in another time. Rat-tat-tat, rat-tat-tat. He nodded as though someone had called his name. For a fleeting moment he saw a woman's face, one that he felt he should have

known, staring up at him wide-eyed and frightened. She went away, she wasn't real, had she ever
been?

Rat-tat-tat, rat-tat-tat, the beat tramped forward
toward him, more strongly now, in purposeful
stride, as though legions of dead were coming for
him. A faint light grew large in his eyes. Then
faded. The drums withdrawing to a distance, still
there but softer now, more friendly, comforting.
He knew that soon they would come again in all
their strength, taking him away to. . . ?

Lim paced his hut, lashing himself with accusa-
tions, questions of right and wrong riddling his
mind as he considered the whimpering, mewling
creature that was Reider. Lim knew that he had
broken all the rules, and the knowledge of his
hideous act tortured him. He tried to avoid
Reider, but the befouled and ragged prisoner followed him about as though he wanted to be near
him. Reider's actions tormented Lim further.

The rains ended. Lim watched Reider crawl
under the poles of Lim's long house to sleep. As he
stretched his aching frame upon the ground,
Reider's fingers made a steady rat-tat-tat upon the
ground. It continued until he fell asleep.

The villagers and soldiers became uneasy in
Reider's presence, pretending not to see him as he
scrambled toward them on his hands and knees.
Disgusted with the man-beast, the villagers began
to regard Lim with a deep dissatisfaction that
approached loathing.

Lim had watched Reider from his window for the last few days, examining minutely every movement his prisoner made. Lim took no food during this time, harshly demanding that he be left alone. The more he concentrated, the more fascinated he became. He could almost feel everything that Reider felt. His body would move and jerk at times, imitating the creature outside, as Reider crawled and begged and warred with the dogs over scraps and bones. His hair, long and tangled, was matted with clots of filth, crawling with vermin that fed off the filth of his body. His beard stuck to his face in tangled knots. He clawed at his scraps with hands that were twisted and bony, kneeling on knees that were swollen disproportionately.

Reider could race along the streets on all fours with a speed that was almost equal to that of the dogs. As Lim watched, a great draining sense of self-revulsion overwhelmed him. He could take no more. Reider's suffering had become a reflection of his own soul.

Lim stood before the mirror and studied the figure reflected there, noting the clean uniform and polished boots. He straightened his tunic as his orderly fastened the pistol belt around his waist. Then he turned and walked out of the long house, down the log steps to the spot where Reider sat, tapping his fingers in the dust and gently, rythmically nodding his head. The sun threw their sharp shadows to one side of them; it was two o'clock. The village was quiet. A plane had passed overhead an hour ago, but the silence had reigned since then.

"Sergeant Reider!" Lim spoke softly. "Do you hear me?"

Reider did not reply, but simply stared ahead, nodding, as his fingers tapped the dust repeatedly.

"Sergeant Reider!" Lim shouted. "I am sorry! Do you hear what I am saying to you? I am sorry! Do you hear me? I am sorry! This is the only act of my life for which I feel shame! I was wrong, I know this! But you must understand why I did such a thing. You drove me to it!"

"Why could you have not surrendered to me and saved so many months of torment for both of us? If you had given in, stopped fighting me, I would have sent you north to be with your comrades till this war is over! But, no, you pushed me till I had no choice! So now we reach the end, Sergeant! There is no longer any need to put you or myself through this!"

Reider's fingers tapped on, his head nodding slightly to the rat-tat-tat beside his leg.

"Do you hear me, Sergeant? It is over! It is time to end this! No more! Do you hear me? I can't take any more of you! I am sorry!"

With his one good arm, Lim reached across his body to open the flap of his holster. The snap unfastened and Reider sprang.

With a ululating groan, Reider struck Lim with all the reserves remaining in his body, driving Lim backwards, seizing the gun, shooting Lim through the throat. Lim fell upon his back as great gouts of bright arterial blood rose from the gaping wound to the throb of his pulse and the boot heels that thudded upon the dry earth. As the air rattled out of his torn esophagus, the darkness closed in, and in it he heard himself saying softly, as he'd done as a child kneeling before the priest, "Forgive me, father, for I know that I have sinned." But it was the ancient dark spirits of his blood, the Than Tien, the spirits of the mountains, who came at last and claimed him.

Reider turned and raised his eyes unblinking into the fierce white heat of the Cambodian sun.

"I am not an animal," Reider muttered distinctly.

And from deep within him, once again, the rat-tat-tat of the drums beat toward through his brain, even as the burst of machinegun fire from behind him pierced his back with such force that his chest was torn from him. But there was no sense of pain or loss as Reider's spirit moved away to the rat-tat-tat of the hell-born drums, leaving the tortured frame behind him. The sounds of firing came from all around him, cries of pain and fear swelled as machinegun fire and mortars smashed huts and bodies, cutting down the VC in packs. Reider heard only the call of the drums. Rat-tat-tat . . . rat-tat-tat. . . .

Sizemore stood over what remained of Reider, his eyes going from Lim to his friend. It was nearly impossible to recognize the bleeding thing at his feet, lying on its face, the body twisted, clawed hands dug into the dry earth. Sizemore paid no attention to the fighting going on around him as the Mike Force mopped up. There was too much lying there in the dust for him to see anything else. He knelt leaning over the body to look at the face, unaware of the tears running down his own face, dropping to mix with the blood of what had been a man.

Wearily, he rose to his feet, his grip tightening on his submachinegun. So softly that Williams could not hear him, although he was standing at his shoulder, he whispered: "Thank God, we were too late. . . ."

Best-Selling Horror and Occult from TOR

☐ 48-042-3 **The Wells of Hell** $2.95
Graham Masterton

☐ 48-043-1 **Night Vision** $2.95
Frank King

☐ 48-041-5 **The Possession of** $2.95
Jessica Young
Russ Martin

☐ 48-046-6 **The Playground** $2.95
T.M. Wright

☐ 48-055-5 **The Kill** $2.95
Alan Ryan

☐ 48-054-7 **The Obsession of** $2.95
Sally Wing
Russ Martin

☐ 48-061-X **Tengu** $3.50
Graham Masterton

☐ 48-076-8 **Nightmare Seasons** $2.95
Charles L. Grant

☐ 48-075-X **Shaitan** $3.95
Max Ehrlich

Buy them at your local bookstore or use this handy coupon:
Clip and mail this page with your order